Jill Paton Walsh was educated at St Michael's Convent, North Finchley, and at St Anne's College, Oxford. She is the author of three adult novels: *Lapsing* (1986), *A School For Lovers* (1989) and *Knowledge of Angels* (1994), which was shortlisted for the 1994 Booker Prize. She has also won many awards for her children's literature, including the Whitbread Prize, the Universe Prize and the Smarties Award.

She has three children and lives in Cambridge.

Praise for *A School For Lovers*:

'An ingenious celebration of Mozart ... An entertaining dance through self-deception to real feeling ... Artful in the best sense, enriched by fine descriptive writing and by a thoroughgoing addiction to the opera in question'
Guardian

'An elegant and witty tribute to the genius of Mozart ... The beauty and grace, artifice and skill of the work ... A charming Renaissance conceit'
Opera Now

'Pacy narrative, strong visual sense, directness of tone, clarity of style'
Times Literary Supplement

'A light, witty novel about the risks of falling in love. The novel works as Shakespearian comedy, an operetta with majestic settings, quicksilver changes in emotion, an amused but sympathetic tone and the belief that young love is too naïve and transitory to be tragic'
Financial Times

Also by Jill Paton Walsh

KNOWLEDGE OF ANGELS
LAPSING

and published by Black Swan

A SCHOOL
FOR LOVERS

Jill Paton Walsh

BLACK SWAN

A SCHOOL FOR LOVERS
A BLACK SWAN BOOK : 0 552 99646 7

Originally published in Great Britain by
George Weidenfeld & Nicolson Ltd

PRINTING HISTORY
Weidenfeld & Nicolson edition published 1989
Black Swan edition published 1996

Set in 11pt Linotype Melior by
County Typesetters, Margate, Kent.

Black Swan Books are published by Transworld Publishers Ltd,
61–63 Uxbridge Road, Ealing, London W5 5SA,
in Australia by Transworld Publishers (Australia) Pty Ltd,
15–25 Helles Avenue, Moorebank, NSW 2170
and in New Zealand by Transworld Publishers (NZ) Ltd,
3 William Pickering Drive, Albany, Auckland.

Reproduced, printed and bound in Great Britain by
Cox & Wyman Ltd, Reading, Berks.

La mia Dorabella capace non è

Cosi Fan Tutte, Act I, sc. i, l. i.

'My Dora couldn't do such a thing,' says Ferdy. And Alfie laughs. He laughs outright and with an edge of spite, so that the two young men suddenly glimpse that possible unpleasant side of Alfie, of which, it must be said, they have been warned.

Nevertheless the second of them speaks up. 'Neither could my Fleur,' he says. 'It's unthinkable.'

Alfie looks up. The sherry decanter poised in his hand freezes at the fulcrum between pouring and not pouring, with a golden bead on its brim. 'Ah,' he says. 'Well, my dears, it's a shame to quarrel over it. I speak with the wisdom of age, but not with any intention to annoy.'

Ferdy, however, *is* annoyed. 'That's not good enough, Alfie,' he says. 'It's too bad of you, slandering a young woman with whom you are perfectly unacquainted, against whom you can know nothing, just because you are disappointed, because one of your little schemes has come unstuck.'

'On the contrary, darling, it is too bad of *you*,' says Alfie, 'to deny me my pleasures on such piffling grounds, when I have done so much for you, and I was looking forward to it!'

Alfie finishes pouring sherry – just one glass – and, sitting in his huge fireside armchair, begins to sip it himself.

William, sitting in the window-seat, looks gloomily across the preposterous splendours of the quadrangle, which assert in brick and stone a measured and reasonable vision of the world, a tangible optimism. As he often does when things go wrong, he runs a rapid retake through his mind of the last few hours, looking for the moment of error. He still expects to be able to take back his mistakes as soon as he spots them. It had been a bright day, the road conditions had been good, he had made good time to Oxford. He had hauled his trunk up the staircase to his room, and gone at once in search of Ferdy, to shout, and greet, and ask about the vacation, the usual questions, expecting the usual vacuous answers, and with his own news burgeoning, ready to spill out. It was to be told only to Ferdy, that he had firmly resolved. And he had found almost immediately that Ferdy had likewise resolved to tell only him; as shyly as girls they had breathed the two girls' names.

'You can't imagine . . .' Ferdy had said.

'Oh, but I can; by analogy with my own!'

They had both, in the Easter vacation, got engaged.

'How absurdly unlike you, William!' was Ferdy's comment. 'How conventional. The taming of the gay dog.'

'It's no more unlike me than it is unlike you,' retorted William, aiming a mock blow. 'I'm amazed.'

'I didn't think it would surprise you,' said Ferdy solemnly.

'Why not? Why ever not?'

'I thought you would have seen it in *The Times*.'

'You put it in *The Times*?'

'So that my English friends would see it. Don't you read *The Times*? Should I have put in the *Sun*?'

William laughed. 'Well, I might have seen it *there*. I have only read the born, hitched, wed, and dead page in *The Times* once in my life, and that was the other day, looking for myself.'

The summons from Alfie, deckle-edged and exquisitely penned, was propped on the mantelpiece. So at six they had strolled side by side across the quad to Alfie's room, their slightly flamboyant stride and obvious togetherness influenced by knowing that Alfie would be watching from his window, gloating, and would comment, very probably, on how deliciously to advantage young men showed when viewed from above against the eternal cobble and pavement.

William had thought himself up to the minute without finding his mistake; unless it was cooperating with Alfie in the first place. In which case it was Ferdy's error too. They were Alfie's chosen favourites, and outrage was one of his chosen modes of talk. That Alfie should have taken up Ferdy was natural enough; the improbability of his smiling on William caused William considerable amazement. Ferdy was dark and magnificently handsome, smoothed by birth and schooling, and commanding sums of money which frightened William. He was casually generous with it, as an alternative to having to bother about the scale of William's resources.

William would not have put himself in Ferdy's way, had the college not assigned them to a shared room in their first year. They had become immediately fast friends, for each of them – provided that only the other was there to witness it – was capable of the sin of seriousness, and glad now and then to talk earnestly without fear of being mocked. Alfie had taken them as he found them, and he had found them as a pair.

Alfred Lightdown, tutor in musicology, which subject neither of his acolytes studied, was famous, or notorious, in the college. He lived a mildly scandalous life, combining exhibitionism with hedonism, and an antiquarian snobbery developed to the point of lunacy and shamelessly professed. From each of the golden generations rapidly succeeding each other in his select and selective college he chose a few, two or three, as disciples. Alfie's chosen, burnished by the abrasive flow of his conversation, by opera parties, excursions in appreciation of ecclesiastical architecture, and visits to the glamorous houses and clubs of their predecessors, duly shone. The chosen of many generations – for Alfie had been long ensconced – now occupied positions in public life, politics, the arts, the diplomatic service, and tended to feel avuncular sympathy for new recruits. Self-interest and enjoyment alike enjoined the chosen to cooperate; for rumour had it that if thwarted Alfie could be vicious; that he was as influential as an enemy as he was as a friend. Rumour seemed entirely credible in this. And William and Ferdy, like others before them, had received warnings.

But the price to be paid was not what it was rumoured to be by the jealous and malicious unchosen majority; though he showered his young men with endearments, Alfie never touched. In return for all he gave he asked only a little, and that little was of something in which they were so rich that they hardly noticed the imposition. For to young men straight from school the liberty of undergraduates seemed endless. Alfie did rather take you over; you found often that you were whisked away on some outing or special treat. Little by little the student society meetings were missed for whole terms, the subscriptions lapsed, friendship with the unchosen attenuated from neglect. But there was, after all, so much time – enough to work hard, and to train for sporting glory. Alfie liked firsts and blues when possible. And he was usually both tactful and shrewd, avoiding refusals and frustrations with considerable skill. That he is pressing them now against the grain of their inclinations is unprecedented. As well as unpleasant.

For the conversation has certainly taken an unpleasant turn. When they arrived Alfie had adumbrated a delectable excursion, and demanded that they keep the day free, ten days hence, for it. They are both perfectly free and unencumbered, and have said so before they have heard the nature of the excursion, thus depriving themselves of the easy excuse. It is to be a boat trip, going from Folly Bridge early in the morning, with baskets of good food and wine, to reach by evening a riverside garden full of roses, in which a moonlit dance is to be held, in a lamplit marquee, and to which, with difficulty, Alfie hints, he has contrived to get them all invited.

'Why you are not perfectly and utterly happy in each other's society I will never know,' he says. 'But knowing your curious tastes I have provided us with women; young things in the first flush of youth who will tread the greensward with you, and to whom you may fetch strawberries and wine, and who will understand perfectly what will later be expected.'

'My dear Alfie,' says Fernando, 'I can't possibly

take a girl to a dance like that now that I am engaged.'

'You are not serious, my dear,' says Alfie.

'But I am. Surely you can see. How can I get betrothed and go on a blind date in the same month, Alfie?'

'Well, then, William,' says Alfie, 'it seems that you and I must go without him, and between us manage to entertain the naiads. Doubtless we can contrive it, though we must take turn and turn about, since the pleasure of dancing with me can be overstated.'

'I'm very sorry, sir,' says William. 'But I, too . . . I am engaged as well . . . I don't feel that I can either . . .'

'But I have already invited the young women!' cries Alfie. 'Am I to *snub* them? You must come!'

'You must find them other partners,' says Ferdy.

'The whole point was the pleasure of being with you,' says Alfie. 'And I find you incomprehensible. You are engaged – so there shall be no more cakes and ale! How utterly moral, how dismally middle class! What harm will it do?'

'If you don't see, I really don't think I can explain it,' says Ferdy, stiffly.

'And where are they, these prefects of fidelity, to whom you have sworn yourselves? Are they living in Kidlington and Headington, and watching the roads out of Oxford? Are they posted on Folly Bridge, watching who takes boats on the river?'

'It's a weird coincidence,' William tells him. 'They are both working at a house called Roseguard, though they live in different counties . . . we are hoping they will meet and like each other.'

'But if they are not here, why need they know?' cries Alfie. 'We shall have our little joy-ride.'

'No,' says Ferdy.

'But you don't suppose that they will be turning

12

down dances for you? They will be cavorting with anyone who offers, while you sit alone in dreary propriety . . . they're all bitches; they all run with every dog.'

'My God, Alfie,' says Ferdy. 'If you say that sort of thing about her I think I'll thrash you. Take it back.'

An expression of cunning crosses Alfie's face. 'But what if I can prove it?' he says. 'What if I can demonstrate that within a week of being at Rose-guard your girls will not only dance with, but sleep with, other men. Can I have my party then?'

'My girl's not capable of it,' says Ferdy.

'Will you take a bet on it?' Alfie asks.

'Alfie . . .'

'Will you take a bet?'

'I will bet my life on Fleur's good faith,' says William.

'Foolish boy. But luckily no-one wants such a forfeit; I am betting you each ten thousand pounds that if we put them to the test we will find them willing to have a little fun on the side . . . while the cat's away, so to speak . . .'

'Make it a hundred thousand, if you like!' says Ferdy.

'Now I know you are fooling, Alfie,' says William. 'You know I could never afford to bet any such sum; as long as I live I don't expect to have that sort of money to hazard, and besides, I am engaged; I shall have to provide; we shall have houses and children to think of.'

'But a bet doesn't have to be symmetrical, dear boy. That would be very unfair as between a rich old rotter like me, and a young sprig such as you; I am betting you that if you will submit to my instruc-tions, and carry them out faithfully to the letter, your girls will prove to be just like the rest – ten thousand pounds to twenty. Yes or no?'

13

'Yes!' says Ferdy. 'You're on!'

'Both, or neither,' says Alfie. 'What does William say?'

'He's taking it, too,' says Ferdy. 'I'll talk him into it.'

When they leave, Alfie moves into his dressing room. Being inserted in a projecting jut of the building, and high up, it commands a good view of the indigo dusk, and the golden lamplight in the quad. He watches them walking away without pleasure, indeed with an expression that suggests a sudden onset of disgust. Glancing at a little silver-framed photograph on the massive chest of drawers he says to it, 'It's truly astonishing, don't you think? that generation after generation these callow mediocrities expect to enjoy perfect love – take it as their birthright, indeed – when the best of their elders and betters cannot have it.'

The photograph offers no confirmation, and Alfie twitches the curtain closed across the darkening scene outside, before the young men are out of sight.

'But don't you see? He hasn't a chance! We shall win easily,' Ferdy says, as he walks with William back across the quadrangle. 'It's a shame to take the poor old duffer's money, really. Perhaps we should be more scrupulous . . . but I take it you could use ten thousand?'

'Use it?' says William. 'I can hardly bear to think what it would do for us . . . down payment on a mortgage . . . no waiting and scrimping . . . it would make things much easier with her father.'

'Well, then?'

'But have you thought it through, Ferdy? You really mean us to try to seduce each other's girl?'

'We'll have to try reasonably hard, won't we?' says

14

Ferdy, 'because we'll be on our honour. I mean, we can hardly take the bet, and then deliberately fix the outcome. That would be almost theft. Cheating, certainly. Do you object to trying? Granted that you have my permission?'

'And your assurance that I shall fail?'

'Of course you will fail. Then do you object to my passionately laying siege to your Fleur?'

'How could I object, when I know you won't get anywhere?'

'Then we shall scrupulously carry out our undertaking to Alfie, so that we can take his money with clear consciences. We shall try as hard as we can, in the circumstances. If it fails to convince the girls, it won't be for want of trying. Agreed?'

'But . . . ought one to try to find out something which, if it's true, one wouldn't at all like to know, Ferdy? It feels to me as though a folk-tale vengeance might be attached to it.'

'But, William, I do know it. I do know she can love only me. She says so; and a person such as she is could not possibly . . . Have you any doubts at all, for your part?'

'Of course not!'

'Then we must win. Alfie's nasty cynicism will cost him dear. Where's the flaw? We shall win, and throw a huge party to celebrate!'

'And shall we invite Alfie?' says William, catching Ferdy's mood, and smiling.

'Naturally. No hard feelings,' Ferdy says.

Though neither William nor Ferdy studied musicology, others did. Mr Alfred Lightdown had hours a week in tutorial sessions with young men and women of his college. He regretted the young

15

women, but the college having gone co-ed some years back, he had no choice. Since this was the Mozart term, it could not be long before someone reading an essay remarked that in *Cosi Fan Tutte* Mozart had inexplicably chosen to set to exquisite music a remarkably silly plot.

'And what,' demanded Alfie, leaning back in his enormous Victorian armchair, and coldly staring at his pupils, 'do you find so particularly silly about it?'

'Those ridiculous disguises,' said Anna at once.

'Well, the whole thing . . .' said Thomas.

'Anna reassures me somewhat,' said Alfie. 'The question of disguises being one on which modern awareness has undoubtedly shifted. You are not alone in finding them incredible, dear girl, though past ages seem to have taken the idea in their stride. Shakespeare is full of them, and he is not commonly accused of rampant silliness, after all.'

'That's different, sir,' said Anna.

'In what way?'

'Well, the disguised characters are characters . . . I mean actors. We can see an actor change costumes before our very eyes. Rosalind is just as much in disguise as Rosalind as she is as Ganymede. Accepting Ganymede isn't very different from accepting Rosalind. The programme notes tell us who it really is . . . but in real life . . .'

'You should remember that the singers in *Cosi* do not appear as themselves, any more than Shakespearian actors do. However, I am interested in your implied contrast with real life. After all, there was a rumour running round Vienna that *Cosi* was based on something that had recently occurred at the court of the Emperor Joseph II, and that he had ordered Mozart to base an opera on it. This clearly seemed more credible to some people than the idea that the divine Mozart had chosen freely to work with such a tale. What do you say to that?'

'There must have been a lot of idiots in Vienna!' said Thomas. 'This story has all the marks of a fairy tale. Not of a happening. I disagree with Anna; the disguises aren't the nub of the matter. Even without them we are being asked to believe that two young women in love would all on the same day be cast into despair at losing their betrothed, be tempted, fall in love again, get to the brink of marriage . . .'

'Just as I feared,' said Alfie. 'A romantic in our midst. I hope, Thomas, you are not telling us you find infidelity improbable?'

'At that speed? Certainly I do.'

'You make me feel my age,' said Alfie, sighing. 'Personally, I would find a tale of lifelong fidelity more implausible by far than the tale in *Cosi*. It is not a fairy tale, strictly, Thomas. Da Ponte got it from somewhere in his beloved Italian poetry. He usually did quarry from that source. I have a quote somewhere . . . yes . . . this is when he was working on *Don Giovanni*: *"At night I shall write for Mozart, and imagine I am reading Dante's Inferno. In the morning I shall write for Martini, and feel as if I'm studying Petrarch. In the evening it will be Salieri's turn, and that shall be my Tasso."*

'The origins of *Cosi* are to be found in *Orlando Furioso*. Try Canto 43. And I cannot resist pointing out to you that last week's discussion of *Don Giovanni* ran the full allotted hour without anyone cavilling at its plausibility, though the hero has deflowered of Spanish ladies one thousand and three. Am I to take it that you find that easier to believe than that two young women are light-of-love? Really?'

They stared at Alfie, baffled. Then, 'I hadn't given the matter any thought at all,' said Thomas, candidly. 'I confess I had dismissed *Cosi* as unworthy of serious consideration on this level, though the music, of course . . .'

'Then perhaps we should take more time to think this through,' said Alfie. 'It raises questions of realism and romanticism at many levels; on stage, in the minds of the characters, and in our own minds.'

'However much time we take, there are still the disguises,' said Anna.

'That I grant you,' said Alfie. 'But they are not, I think, at the heart of things. You are right, Anna, that if one were to conduct any such experiment in present times one would have to dispense with disguises. I am unalarmed; I have thought of a way round them.'

'But . . . ?' said Anna, again staring at Alfie.

'We shall take as much time as we need to plumb the depths of all this,' the tutor said. 'Next week Thomas shall read me an essay on the origins of the story in *Cosi*, and Anna one on literary, musical and magical disguises. *Au revoir*, my dears.'

As the two pupils departed, clattering down the turns of the oak staircase, they heard Alfie in a resonant bass above their heads, singing, *'In Espagna, mille tre, mille tre!'*

They exchanged uneasy glances, going under the arch and into the open sunlight of the quadrangle where the air was laden with perfume from the choice and tender shrubs which generations of gardeners had brought to perfection against the medieval walls. 'Whatever did he mean: "he had thought of a way round" the disguises?' said Anna. 'He gives me the creeps!'

'He's an odd fish, yes, I agree,' said Thomas. 'If one believed all they say about him . . . have you time for a coffee?'

'Thank you, yes,' said Anna, sounding surprised. She was not to know that the very freckles which

18

made her sure she was ugly had enraptured her tutorial partner. He would have called them 'summer voys', and he was susceptible to them. They made him think of harvests in golden fields. The offer of coffee was the first sign he had plucked up courage to offer, since radiant beauty was not, he thought, really within his social scope. But girls who think themselves ugly are genuinely surprised at approaches, even modest ones.

And while they stood, modestly surprised, below his windows, Alfie sang on, his deep voice mingled vibrantly with the scent of magnolia grandiflora, '*voi sapete, voi sapete, voi sapete quel che fa!*'

The house is hard to find. It seems not to be in a village, but solitary, and there are no signposts. Over and over again, Fleur stops the car, and consults the scrawled map provided by the owner. She is cross with herself for not having brought an Ordnance Survey map; the road atlas ignores every one of the narrow lanes she is lost in. When she stops the car birdsong floods into it. The land is flat and verdant, ringed with shadowy hills standing back some miles. The lanes are deep, screened all the way with hedgerows frothing exuberantly with cow parsley, and ragged robin, and odd little patches of bluebell like the cutting scraps of a silk ballgown, like the shimmer of water deep in the tender grass. The lane she is following mounts a gentle slope, and comes out on top with a wide view of the land; crosses a blazing and stinking field of rape, then a rich carpet of young wheat squealing with larksong, and then plunges into a ruined wood, where stag-headed trees stoically support the trunks of their fallen comrades, and broken branches choked with ivy have almost suppressed the mirage of water on the forest floor.

Beyond the wood the lane insouciantly crosses a water splash, bright with kingcups, and narrows even further, so that the leaning panicles of cow parsley on one side nod into the leaning ranks of cow parsley on the other. Fleur stops the car, with the shallows of the stream chuckling against the tyres, and again consults the map. It doesn't seem as unlikely on the map as it does on the ground, and besides, while she stares round she sees the next waymark; – almost hidden under a high tide of blossom, the words 'ROMAN ROAD' on a worn wooden board.

So she drives on, the car brushing between the flowering banks – 'Heaven knows what happens if I meet another car!' she thinks – and the lane rises gently away from the stream and takes suddenly a very un-Roman right turn, leaving her facing a gate-way standing wide. On the left stands a lodge-keeper's cottage, with the windows boarded up and the roof fallen in; an elaborately decorated arch of brick topped off with stone fretwork bridges the entrance, and a wrought-iron screen gate of considerable foliate magnificence stands locked in the open position by the Lilliputian lacing of the lower part with grass and weed. But there is a double track, as of wheels, in the grassed-over avenue beyond, and Fleur drives gingerly forwards, bumping along the driveway in a tunnel of brilliant new leaf, until she comes suddenly to a sweep of gravel, only partly perforated by grass, and a view of the house.

The curious character of the house is at once apparent. In front of her, facing the gravelled terrace, is a beautiful classical front, perfectly sym-metrical, and of balanced proportions, measured to give the scope of seeming grandeur to even such a small 'great house' as this one. Fleur studies it knowledgeably. The height of the windows on each of the three storeys, the thick glazing bars on the windows, the apricot-coloured brick laid in Flemish bond, the stone facings to the window cases, the sweep of steps to the wide doorway, complete with portico and fanlight, and the dome visible above the small central pediment all proclaim the eighteenth century triumphant. Something intangible about the frontage, the weight of the detail, perhaps, in proportion to the whole, the presence of bas-relief decoration in appliqué – those Corinthian pilasters on the ends, those windows topped with ball and point broken pediments like furniture – suggests the architect as a wit, and the entire effect as slightly frivolous, reasonable and manically cheerful. But round the edges and over the skyline of this house project bits of another – carved multiple chimneys, battlemented turrets in Strawberry Hill Gothic, and, disputing the summit with the modest dome, several towers of grim and ancient demeanour, Childe Roland school of inspiration, into which have been built, Fleur thinks, frowning as she tries to pick out distant details against the light, great chunks of carving: gargoyles, armorial bearings and broken inscriptions, jackdawed together to give a glued-on antiquity to what is in fact the newer wing of the house. Mildly curious, she counts the towers and turrets, loses count, and comes to two different totals. 'Oh, come on!' she tells herself, contending with a faint reluctance.

Huge and neglected hedges of yew standing shoulder to shoulder with the house on both ends of the façade prevent access except through the door. Fleur gets out of her car, reaches for the seven-inch key that she has been sent, and plods forward.

There is a marbled hall, a rotunda under the

dome, with faded paintings of putti, up to no good in the clouds, and draped figures gesticulating allegorically. There are pale dove-grey marble columns ringing it round, and a maze set in black and white on the floor. Left and right are vistas of rooms in muted light – the blinds are down all along the front – and beyond the rotunda a staircase of classical design sweeps upwards. Fleur begins to explore. But when she crosses the rotunda and begins to ascend the stair the house suddenly changes; the windows lighting the stair, safely out of sight from the rotunda, are wildly pointed and elaborately Gothic, and each door off the gallery above leads to a room of more romantic character than the one before. Fleur walks into bedrooms with four-posters, with carved and intricate overmantels, with hangings rotted into threads in places, showing in dim and dusty colours scenes from gardens and forests, scenes with dragons, knights in armour, and girls in white garments with unbound, flowing hair. She finds a library, hung with fans of halberds, fans of swords, and with a wrought iron gallery running round its overbearing height, and a twisting stair to ascend to the upper levels of the books. The books are all bound in leather and a smell of dust and old saddlery lingers. All the furniture in the library is under dustsheets. Indeed, the further Fleur penetrates the house the less she can see, till at last she is ascending a turret in which everything is under sheets, and thick with many years of dust. Her sandals leave Friday-prints on the floor. And it is dark where she now walks; she has not passed a window, even one closed by a blind, for several minutes.

So far, her attention has been taken up with carefully noting things that will require working on: fabrics and hangings needing mending, cleaning,

22

restoring; paintings coggled on their stretchers, plasterwork cracked and sagging . . . suddenly she remembers that she is to sleep here, to find a room and stay in it. The concentrated creeps that similar settings have imparted to a hundred horror films suddenly ambush her. She freezes, one hand on the centre column of the spiral stair she is ascending, shivering at the thought. And as if answering her fright the sun suddenly throws on the curving stone wall ahead of her and above her the outline of a sunny window, so that she unfreezes, and goes up a few more stairs, to find herself in the top of one of the towers, in a room brightly lit, uncurtained, unsheeted, and with a pleasant little mullioned window with Gothic lights, offering a view of the garden.

The garden had once been made of bowers and courts of yew. The cow parsley has washed into it like waves at high tide, and engulfed it, so that all but the broadest of its effects is smudged and obscured. Empty basins with creeper-covered stumps in the middle had once, of course, been statued fountains – the sort of thing the builder of the Palladian front had installed; the Scots pines and rampant rhododendrons she can see covering a slope a little way off go more naturally with the romantic part of the house, but the formal, intricate maze of interlocking hidden places, marked out in box and yew, and carpeted with overgrown knot-garden, seem to belong to neither. Is the garden, Fleur wonders, older than the house altogether? Had the Palladian builder demolished some lovely Eliza-bethan house, to which the gardens of yew belonged, and were the fragments she had taken to be phoney, built into the outside of the towers, perhaps chunks of that earliest house, dug up in the garden when the foundations of the Gothic house were being laid? She tries, by descending a little, to find windows which would show her the other aspects of the garden. Twenty minutes later she is back in the window of the tower room, frustrated. The secrecy of the garden has been preserved by those who built the house. From other windows she has gained only views of the roofs and parapets, the dome of the house, and beyond, a prospect of the open undulant countryside outside the garden.

But this, the only vista, is worth a second look. The trough between the avenue of hedges, though white with invading cow parsley, is also shot deeply through on either edge with blue; once there had been beds of blue flowers, an effect of deep dazzle against the inky green of the towering walls of yew. There had been topiary – green creatures marshalled in facing rows, lining the walk like ceremonial guardsmen, though now, their shapes all blurred by growth, they are indecipherable, and full of the sinister pathos of figures of Plasticine or bread dough impulsively squashed by a childish maker. Nature, of course, rather than spite, has worked the ruin. To the left of the topiary avenue, standing back behind a screen of hedge, is a curious building, a dovecote, or perhaps rather a belvedere, for it does have windows, she can just see, all very high up and facing the same way, at right angles to the view back to the house, and it is topped off by a widow's walk. The climbing, toppling ivy has nearly shut off the windows, but will need longer to pull down the viewpoint on the roof. Somewhere in front of the belvedere there is a glimpse of green, a sense of lawns, deeply unmown, and as Fleur watches she sees suddenly another person, another girl, a delicate figure moving in the dappled shade, wearing a sky-blue shirt, and with a straw hat, held by a ribbon, hanging at the nape of her neck.

As though Fleur's startlement had flown the yards between and alerted her, this figure turns towards the house, and stares. Fleur at her high window waves, and the stranger waves back, and begins at once to move through the tangled growth down the avenue towards the house. Fleur rattles down the tower stair, down the easy sweep of the classical stair, and looks for a door to the garden. She finds a way eventually, through the formal rooms of the right wing, and through an orangery on to a terrace below the Gothic front, and there, coming towards her, is the girl with the straw hat. A girl of about her own age, dark and graceful.

'I didn't know there would be anybody,' Fleur says. 'I was told nobody would be here till tomorrow, except the gardeners.'

'I am a gardener,' says the other, holding out her hand. 'I am Dora. Do you know where I am to sleep?'

She too, it appears, has been told to choose a room and settle in. 'Somehow,' she says, 'I supposed there would be people . . . someone here other than just us.'

'There are going to be. I am employed on some delicate restoration; I didn't get the impression I would have to fend for myself; quite the contrary, in fact.'

'And I am to work on the garden. I am to have men to help me, and I understood it was a live-in job, with all found.'

'Well, then, other people will be coming, but they haven't come yet. It looks as if nobody has lived here for some time.'

'That's odd,' says Dora. 'Just as you came through the door there I thought I saw two women looking out at us from one of the towers.'

'Which tower?' asks Fleur, with a return of the creepy feeling.

25

'I'm not sure. Perhaps I imagined it. Are you sure you have looked in all the rooms?'

'Not really. It might take a month to find them all,' says Fleur. 'Come in and see.'

There are rooms Fleur hasn't found. In the basement, for example, where there is a range of kitchens with not a dustsheet in sight, and no dust either. Mysteriously there is a faint smell of fresh baked bread lingering in the kitchen. They remount the stairs, and rush through the splendid bedrooms, throwing back the dustsheets, laughing at each other and inviting each other to choose wilder and wilder rooms: 'This one's yours, then, Dora!' cries Fleur, with a sweep of her arm round the dark red, heavily draped room, with a curtained bed embroidered with elephants and leopards, and furnished in red and gold lacquered chests and tables.

'No, no, yours surely!' Dora replies. 'I'll have the next one,' and she flings open the communicating door, for all these rooms are linked, and have several exits and entrances. The next room is in darkness; they blunder around the shapeless ghostly objects under sheets, and fail to find the strings on the blinds. 'Well, no, perhaps not this one,' Dora says.

'Look all you like; they're all weird and wonderful,' Fleur tells her. 'As far as I explored, that is. I'm sure I didn't ferret out everything; I kept getting confused, and losing count of doors and floors and rooms.'

'Did every bedroom you found have two doors and no locks?' says Dora, shuddering slightly.

''Fraid so. Hitchcock house, this is. Do you want to explore some more?'

'I don't think so. It's getting scary. Just show me what you found.'

And so they find themselves in the tower room, looking through the window on to the prospect of garden, and agree that really, this is the only possible room.

'We could haul a couple of those plain beds from just below up here, and find a table and a lamp,' says Fleur.

'But you must already have chosen it. Do you mind?'

'Sharing? Oh, I'd much rather we did! Unless, of course, you'd rather not.'

'Rather be alone down there among the dust-sheets? You're joking! Besides, I am from a large family, and at home sisters always share.'

'Then be my guest – my sister, rather. Let's get a few things up here, and then I'll drive us to that pub we passed on the way here, and we'll get a meal.'

As they heave their beds, upended to pass round the hub of the spiral stair, struggling with the awkward task, Fleur says, 'I can't think what possessed us to take this ridiculous job.'

'I took it to be near someone,' Dora says. 'My fiancé is at Oxford.'

'Well so did I!' says Fleur, surprised. 'I mean so is mine. How odd.'

'Well, I suppose it isn't quite the oddest thing about all this,' says Dora. 'If this is to be your bed, is it going against the left wall, or the right? I mean, there must be thousands and thousands of young men at Oxford.'

'The left please. Look . . .' Fleur reaches a small leather photograph frame from her handbag, 'this is William. Did you ever see anyone so formidably handsome? Could you ever imagine a more impressive face!'

She is smiling; dissembling a little, ready to pretend she speaks in jest. But Dora takes the photograph, and studies it sweetly and gravely for a gratifyingly long moment, before producing from her own pocket a miniature in an oval locket, a painting of a dark-eyed young man of intent expression, with a high, faintly military collar, holding a flower. 'And this is my Fernando,' she says, holding it out to Fleur. 'And I think they had better be equally handsome, don't you, if we are to be sisters? If there is to be harmony between us.'

Thomas sat bent over his work. But his desk was in a little dormer window commanding a view of the entire quadrangle. Below him on the flagged paths and in and out of the archways to staircases and gardens his fellow-students came and went. Thomas was engaged in copying a stanza into his notebook from an antique Ariosto, in leather-bound folio, profusely illustrated with woodcuts. In any other library the volume would have been in the rare books room, but Thomas had found it in the college library and borrowed it without formality. He liked it; he liked the smell of the paper, and the slight bite of the letters into the creamy thickness of the page. He would not usually have given the figures moving below him a second glance, but he was distracted by the sight of a girl punk, her hair blazing pink and green, her black jacket studded all over, her drainpipe jeans grotesquely tight, whose face caught the light, spangled with sequins and pins . . . the college did boast a female punk student – one Horrible Harry – but it was not she. Did Horrible Harry have friends? But the apparition below was not, it seemed, in quest of Horrible Harry, or of any other undergraduate, but parading rather ostentatiously up and down. Something about her troubled him, plucked at his attention, had him frowning at her, when he wanted, he really did want, to concentrate on the task in hand which was puzzling him. And then some movement she made, something about the way she turned on her heels towards him on the path, made him suddenly realize, and he jumped up from his desk, and raced down the giddying turns of the stair to charge towards the strange figure in the quadrangle, and shout at her – his raised voice causing the porter to glance briefly up at him from the glazed sentry-box at the main gate – 'What have you done, what have you done, what have you done to your hair?'

Anna smiled at him through a dust of golden freckles and the glare of fluorescent sparkles painted on. 'You see?' she said. 'It wouldn't work. It couldn't work; you saw through it at once, and we don't even know each other very well.'

'Your hair . . .' He was beyond self-protecting dissembling, his distress clearly showing, but she seemed not to have attention to spare to wonder why he should mind about it.

'Don't worry,' she said. 'It washes out. But it makes the point, doesn't it?'

'It's so short!' he said, grieving. 'You cut it so short!'

'You recognized me within two minutes at a distance of fifty yards, from two storeys up.'

'Not at first glance,' he confessed.

'But for *Cosi* to work we have to believe those men could waltz around in the same room, at close quarters, under the eye of their beloveds . . . what made you guess?'

'An undisguisable essence.'

'Quit fooling. What was it?'

'Something about how you moved. Come and have some coffee, I want to show you something.'

Soon they were ensconced in his dormer corner, looking together at the Ariosto. He reeled inwardly,

29

for as they bent heads over the lovely page the safety pin in her cheek drew a faint, cool line on his. 'I can't work it out,' he said.

'Nor I,' she said. 'What with the funny print, and its being in Italian. Tell me about it.'

'It's a story,' he said. 'Sit over there and take your coffee, and I'll tell it to you. Well, it's a story inside a story, really, like Chinese boxes, and they go like this. There's a hero called Rinaldo who is travelling about on some quest or other, and he spends the night with a courteous host in a castle in Mantua.' Thomas picks up his notes, and comes to sit opposite Anna in the other of his battered armchairs. 'And the host offers him wine in a cup which will spill at once if someone tries to drink from it whose wife is unfaithful. Rinaldo refuses to try it. He says it is stupid to look for something you don't want to find. He believes his wife is faithful to him, and he could gain nothing by putting it to the test. Then – something interesting – he goes on to say that God has proscribed that kind of certainty even more than he proscribed the Tree of Life.'

'You mean, that's where that line in the opera comes from?'

'Which line?'

'It's Don Alfonso, right at the beginning: "Oh, mad wish to attempt to discover the evil which makes us unhappy" – something like that.'

'I hadn't noticed that. But listen, listen! When Rinaldo won't drink from the cup his host gets all weepy and says he's dead right not to; he himself, the host I mean, had ruined his own happiness for life by testing the fidelity of his wife. Then he tells his own story which goes like this: he had a dearly loved and beautiful wife, but an enchantress called Melissa was in love with him and always pestering him. He kept refusing her, because he wanted to be as faithful to his wife as he knew she was to him. Then Melissa pointed out that he didn't know what his wife would do if he was safely out of the way. So he gives it out that he is going on a long journey. Then Melissa disguises him by magic to look like a certain man from Ferrara, whom he knows to be smitten by his wife's beauty, and he tries wooing her.'

'And what happens? What does she say?'

'At first she refuses him. But he is plying her with wonderful jewels, and gold and rubies, just for one night with her, and at last she says she would gratify him if she could be sure nobody would ever find out. Whereupon, of course, Melissa switches him back into his own shape, and he accuses her. Hang on, I want to read you the next bit word for word . . . "Great was her shame, but greater still her anger at the way I had abused her . . ." – get that! – anyway she ups and leaves him at once, and runs off with the guy from Ferrara, and she has been living with him since in pure delight. Rinaldo, hearing all this, says he thinks his host behaved worse in tempting the wife than she did in succumbing so soon. Now, what do you think?'

'Well, we know Da Ponte knew and loved Italian literature, and so obviously he knew Ariosto, and so this is where the *Cosi* story comes from. What's the problem?'

'But is this the same story? Are two stories the same if they are contrived to mean something completely different? And this really does say something very different from *Cosi*, doesn't it?' Thomas's voice had become suddenly shaky. For during the conversation his reaction to Anna's transformation had rapidly changed. The shock had worn off. And though he could manage to keep his desire to touch her under control when she

31

appeared as a respectable fellow-student, chastely dressed and smoothly combed, as for sitting alone with her when she was togged up like a wild and decadent easy-rider . . . he suddenly lurched forward, and kneeling in front of her armchair seized her, and began to tear open the press-studs that closed her abominable jacket. Somewhere in the back of his mind he expected his assault to be rewarded with a karate chop, or wrestler's throw, so convincing was her alter ego; but when gradually he realized that he had knocked the safety pin off, and got her half naked without meeting any resistance, he went watery at the knees, and groaning, half dragged, half carried her through to the tiny bedroom, the narrow bed.

She, meanwhile, was at first curious and amused, perhaps influenced herself by her disguise, her transformed body language; and then, seeing the state he was in, she became ravenous for his relief, triumphant in its achievement. A light breeze through the window in the next room mellifluously rustled and turned the pages of the Ariosto, changing the place in the book.

'I love you,' said Thomas. 'Oh, God, I love you! I shall love you for ever and ever and ever, and if I stopped I would die!'

'I'm feeling skittish,' says Dora. 'I can't wait for Ferdy to turn up; – he promised he would. I'm dying to show him all this.'

'William said he would come over as soon as he could,' says Fleur. 'We might take a bit of finding in this set-up, in the house, or the garden. I think I shall start working where I will be right in view of the front door – on those little carvings in the hall.'

But she has hardly begun work, getting ready her brushes and sponges, when she hears a car on the crunchy gravel of the drive. Her heart leaping, she goes to the door, and opens it, just as Dora appears from the garden round a screen of yew. They are both disappointed. The car produces Alfie.

'My dear young ladies, brace yourselves for bad news,' he says. 'I know you don't know me; I am a friend of William, and of Fernando. I'm afraid there has been a calamity.'

'William hurt?' says Fleur, suddenly holding on to the nearest pillar of the portico.

'Ferdy?' says Dora.

'A terrible accident,' says Alfie. 'I hardly know how to tell you . . . a dreadful fall . . . poor young men!'

'For pity's sake!' cries Dora. 'Are they ill, injured, dead? Tell us!'

'Dead?' says Alfie, putting an avuncular arm round Dora's shoulder – she has approached him, spellbound in dismay – and leading her up the steps towards her trembling friend. 'Of course not! Nothing so terrible, but bad enough all the same. Both of your fiancés must leave, at once, indefinitely.'

Whereupon from shock, dismay and relief, both girls burst into tears.

Alfie consoles them. He leads them into a golden gallery, throws back dustsheets, installs them facing him on an elegant settee, finds in an elaborate inlaid cabinet a little whisky, and some fine, twist-clouded Venetian glasses, and administers comfort. Then he begins to explain himself.

A climbing accident, he tells them, has taken the lives of two of the men of his college – William and Ferdy's college, at which he is a tutor. This has produced, at the last minute, a need to call on the reserve volunteers for an expedition to St Kilda which the tutor in Natural History is leading. Of course, when they put their names down for this adventure neither of the young men had foreseen becoming engaged – 'How could anyone foresee, dear young ladies, the impact of beauty such as yours?' – but the fact is they cannot decently withdraw the moment they are needed, having shared all the briefing and training that has gone on in the previous year.

'How long are they going for?' asks Dora.

'Six months in the first instance. A possible further six months depending on the progress the programme achieves.'

'And can we see them to say goodbye?' asks Fleur.

'Would they have sent me if that were possible?' says Alfie. 'This very moment,' – he looks at his watch – 'they are on a coach to Portsmouth, where the boat awaits them. But I have brought you each a letter, and if you can write at once, I can undertake to put your answers in the express packet of last-minute things which a courier is taking down to the docks, and which will probably be in time.' He looked again at his watch. 'I can give you half an hour, to write,' he says.

Each girl taking her own letter, they leave him, seeking solitude in a house that seems, for all its size and emptiness, not to offer it.

'I'm not such a bad actor,' says Alfie, *sotto voce*, in a satisfied tone. He strolls along the gallery, looking idly at the murky paintings and muffled furniture, with an expression of faint distaste. 'Gloriosities,' he says, 'merely.' At the end of the gallery he throws open a door, and emerges on to the terrace below the Gothic front. From a window above his head he can hear, faintly – but sound carries in the sunlit silence – someone sobbing quietly. He cannot tell which girl it is, but then it is a matter of perfect indifference to him which is which. But it is just as well that neither William nor Ferdy is within earshot. He sighs, thinking ruefully, yearningly, of the tough and ruthless acolytes enjoyed by Don Alfonso of the opera, who could even risk bringing his young men on stage to take leave of the girls face to face, to make them cry and not at once admit it was a lie that they were going anywhere; whereas he had to make do with a pair who could not be trusted to perpetrate a moment's unkindness, even for the king's ransom on offer, and not because they would refuse the proposition on principle, but because they would lack the necessary self-control. Then, struck by another thought, he strides rapidly back into the building, and goes in search of the kitchens.

Half an hour later, holding the precious letters, he tells the two, as they stand, all three, in the smooth web of the intricate maze on the rotunda floor, 'You must not think, my dears, of the expedition as a horrible ordeal. It is a good life, I am told. Plenty of variety, lots of challenge, no two days the same, and always with the hope of fame and glory if they discover something new to science. It isn't even as dangerous as you might think; they expect to survive it! Apart from the chance of shipwreck – quite remote, these days – they do nothing more dangerous than rock-climbing.'

Watching his car sweep away down the avenue, Fleur says, 'What a loathsome man!'

'But surely it was very kind of him,' says Dora, 'to fetch and carry letters for us – for them.'

'But I thought,' says Fleur, 'I thought he was actually enjoying bringing bad news; didn't you?'

While Alfie, parked in a sea of cow parsley half a mile away, where the thickly blossoming quickthorn of the hedgerow screens him from the house, is tearing open their letters and reading them. His harsh laughter is lost in the racket set up by the smutty circling birds in the rookery in the nearby trees.

My dearest, dearest Will,

I would rather die than live without you. This disaster, this sudden parting brings that home to me. Of course it is not your fault that you have to go. I know you would never willingly do anything to hurt me, and I will not reproach you, though this causes me such pain. I think I did not until this minute know what unhappiness really was! I only ask you to love me faithfully while you are far away. Write to me every day. I shall be fearful every minute of every hour that you may be in danger, in case separation is not the worst that might happen. For my sake, take care of yourself! May the winds be gentle, and the waters calm for your journey, may all the rocks of that distant island be sunlit and safe for you – may everything go well for you, dearest love.

Your adoring,
Fleur

Darling Ferdy,

I write to you in sorrow that we are to be parted. Of course I understand that in the circumstances you have been forced to go, but the time will be terrible without you, like being dead, dead certainly to any contentment or delight. Of course this will put off the date of our wedding. And I do not know how soon another propitious date may occur . . . so we are cheated of our hopes in this harsh world; such misfortunes make it hard to make any

*plans, or to allow oneself to trust in any hopes.
At least I shall hope that you will write to me as
often as you can – several times a day! – and
keep me faithfully in your thoughts.*

   Your loving betrothed,
   Dora

'Obviously you have read these, Alfie,' says
William coldly, 'since they come without envelopes.
So you surely must realize now . . .'

'Are you still saying what you said before, Alfie,
now you have seen them, now you have read these
words?' says Ferdy. He holds the folded letter close
to his heart, and his eyes are moist.

'Wait and see, my friends,' says Alfie. 'Wait and
see. The last act crowns the play.'

But looking over their letters again in their own
room, they wince.

'We must stop this at once, Ferdy,' says William.
'Look what pain we have inflicted; we are being
both stupid and cruel. I can't think why I agreed.'

'Somehow, knowing myself that it was foolery, I
had not foreseen how seriously it would grieve her,'
says Ferdy. 'But I don't see how we can get out of it
now.'

'Oh, I'm not afraid of Alfie!' says William. 'I shall
just go and tell him the bet's off, and to hell with
him.'

'No, wait.' Ferdy puts his letter carefully into his
wallet, and strides up and down in agitation. 'Think
about it, William!'

'I have thought. I am ashamed to have let myself
be led into such unkindness.'

'It's for an awful lot of money.'

'That only makes it worse!'

'But we have inflicted the pain already, and shall have to answer for it. But if we back off now we shan't have anything to show for it.'

'The hell with the money!' cries William.

'No, think. Think how it will seem to them. We bet on their fidelity; we let Alfie tell them we are going off for months, and then when it's too late to prevent upsetting them over that thought we back off without putting anything actually to the test; if you were them, what would you think we were up to?'

'I don't follow you; what are you saying?'

'That if we back down now it will look – it must look – as though we are having second thoughts about trusting them.'

William, who already had his hand on the doorknob, on his way to Alfie, stops, returns to the armchair, and sits down.

'Supposing one of them said to one of us,' Ferdy continues, '"we could easily have won all that money and got married at once if only you had trusted me," then what do we say? We can hardly say we held back for fear of giving them pain; not now.'

'They are going to be furious with us, when they find out,' says William miserably.

'But when we win, they will be both gloriously vindicated and rich! Whereas, if we back out now . . .'

'All right. I see what you mean. But would they need to know? Couldn't we just lie a little? Say the expedition was cancelled, or they found we had flat feet, or something?'

Ferdy shakes his head. 'Alfie would tell all. He knows where to find them. And Alfie would be furious with us.'

The two young men sit staring at each other gloomily from chairs on either side of the unlit gas fire. 'We've just got to go through with it, haven't we?' says William at last.

'Well, we shouldn't over-react,' says Ferdy. 'All we've done is to give the impression, for a few days at most, that they won't be seeing us for a while. I mean, is that really so dreadful? And cheer up, old chap, we're going to win; we are certainly going to win!'

The tutorial was going well. So it seemed to Anna, sitting on Alfie's deeply cushioned sofa, in a beam of light angled through his windows, and dappled by the leaves of the morning glories growing on his balcony. Thomas sat beside her, reading his essay, and Alfie, glass in hand, prowled the room listening.

The glass contained champagne, which the tutor was generously sharing with them, and which Anna was enjoying; it tasted wonderful, and tickled the back of her nose. Thomas's full glass was quietly fizzing beside him, and she could see the tiny flying fragments of the miniature explosions in the liquid catching the light just above the rim of the glass. She had expected to know what would be in Thomas's essay, having heard the Rinaldo story, but he had burrowed further back still.

'The tale in Ariosto is really only a beefed-up version of an incident in the story of Cephalus and Procris in Ovid's *Metamorphoses*,' Thomas read, 'as the following paraphrase makes clear: Cephalus, carried off by the Goddess Aurora, resists her, pleading the love he feels for his wife, Procris. Aurora angrily sends him back to his wife, telling him he will come to wish he had never clapped eyes on her. This makes Cephalus afraid that Procris has been unfaithful to him. Disguised by Aurora, he

39

goes home incognito, and finds a quiet and orderly house, full of grief for the absence of the master. Instead of being content, he offers Procris greater and greater gifts for a night in her arms, until she hesitates; whereupon he declares himself, and accuses her. Procris flees from the home where she has been tricked, and takes to the woods. Cephalus tries to win her back, vainly until he confesses that he himself was in the wrong, and that he too would have fallen into the same fault had he been offered such gifts.'

'I thought Cephalus and Procris was about how she rustled about in the bushes when he was hunting, and he put an arrow through her,' said Anna.

'Later on,' Thomas told her. 'A separate incident, as Ovid tells it. Anyway, we do know that Da Ponte knew his Ovid as well as his Ariosto, because he wrote some poems about Philemon and Baucis, which are certainly based on Ovid. But about *Cosi* I am not really sure. I think it more likely that the direct source drawn on by Da Ponte was the retelling of Cephalus and Procris in Boccaccio's *Famous Women*.'

'Oh, really?' said Alfie, looking, for the first time that morning, interested. 'You are not drinking, Thomas. Champagne is wasted on those who let it go flat. Now, why do you say that? The versions in Boccaccio and in Ovid are more or less identical, aren't they, and the Ariosto only the same thing tricked out a bit with medieval claptrappery. How can we tell which version Da Ponte used?'

'I expect he knew them all, really,' said Thomas. 'But it's a very moot point whether they are all the same. After all, to be the same story two versions have to have the same moral impact, don't they? It's not enough just that they contain a similar incident.

Let me read you my paraphrase of the Boccaccio version: Cephalus pretends to go on a long journey, returns and tempts Procris through go-betweens. She consents, he reveals himself. Full of shame and troubled conscience because of her misdeeds, she flees into the woods. You see?'

But both Alfie and Anna were staring blankly at him.

'The point I am making, sir, is that this version, like *Cosi*, entirely lacks the sense that there is anything wrong in conducting the test in the first place; it entirely lacks the condemnation of the man for wanting certainty, for mistrust, for resorting to trickery, the sense that the infidelity, far from being the underlying true state of the woman's heart, has been created by the ruse that purported to discover it.'

'Wait a minute,' said Alfie. 'I'm not sure I grasp the distinction you are making. And I do so enjoy learning from my pupils; I enjoy comic reversals.'

'I am making a distinction between versions which treat the woman as wronged and provoked by being subjected to test, and versions which assume that if she fails it the test was justified. I would regard versions of the latter kind as somewhat morally obtuse. And *Cosi* is definitely of the latter kind. Or at least, the libretto is.'

'You amaze me!' said Alfie. 'You are in the grip of a fallacy called shooting the messenger. A person detected in crime will naturally blame the detective; the woman who is light-of-love will naturally set up an uproar about the iniquity of reading someone else's letters, making propositions in disguise, coming home early, or whatever . . . but the essence of all these versions is the same. It is that women are universally unfaithful, and only fools think otherwise. Now you were making, I think, an interesting

41

further observation, if I understood you correctly. Rinaldo declines to drink the magic cup, you told us, because if his wife is unfaithful he would rather not know. But you are suggesting, I think, not that it would be best not to know if your dear one is unfaithful, but that if you make no attempt to find out, she will actually *be* faithful . . . is that the point you were making?'

'It is what I was finding implied in Ariosto.'

'We will need more than a faint implication in an ancient author to bring us to disbelieve something which all adult experience conclusively validates,' said Alfie. 'Women just are unfaithful. *Cosi fan Tutte!*'

Thomas turned to Anna, and said to her directly, 'You know, the libretto does leave the men blameless. It never for a moment suggests shooting the messenger. But the music says something else altogether.'

At which Alfie too, addressed Anna. 'Believing in faithful love is like believing in Father Christmas; one grows out of it. Doesn't one, young Anna?'

'I suppose so,' said Anna, reluctantly. 'I suppose you're right, but I hope you're wrong.'

'But I am not wrong, my dear young lady. I am confident that I am right. However, Thomas here does demonstrate something to me with stunning clarity. The seepage of romanticism into rational belief is remorseless. The theorem that women are incapable of fidelity doesn't stay proved. A demonstration is needed, over and over again.'

'But, sir,' said Thomas, 'it isn't the kind of thing that could stay proved. If one woman vacillates, that proves nothing about others. However many times some woman is unfaithful we cannot conclude that any individual woman will also . . .'

'However many times the sun rises in the east, we

42

must not feel certain that it will do so tomorrow morning!' said Alfie. 'Ho, ho! I have you figured, Thomas. What a heart you have! You would go hunting the wind with a butterfly net, you would!'

'How good that smells!' The speaker is wearing a nurse's uniform, and sitting comfortably in a large Windsor chair. The young woman she speaks to is stirring a pot on the immense range which dominates a kitchen looking like an exhibit in a museum, except for the discordant modern packets of groceries on the handiest shelf.

'It's the chocolate you can smell. *Petits pots au chocolat.* Let's have some!' says the cook, reaching for a ladle. 'Why should we confine ourselves to the smell, while the clients get the substance? I suppose our taste buds are as good as theirs. You're supposed to let this set in little ramekins, but it is delicious hot with bread!' She sets two bowls of the fragrant dark confection on the table, and a basket with several chunks of new-made bread.

'It's wonderful!' says the nurse. 'I suppose you wouldn't be able to cook for us now and then, while you are here?'

'All the time, if you like. I've been given a budget that would banquet an army. All to be lavished on two young women employed here – nothing but the best for them! Certainly we'll look after ourselves while we're about it.'

'It's very strange, you know, Rosemary,' says the nurse. 'Nothing has been done here for at least twenty years, and the owner hardly ever comes; and then suddenly . . .'

'More than twenty years, I should think, judging by the time it took to get the kitchen up and running!

Call me Roz. And as for strange, you can say that again! I'm supposed to inveigle myself into the clients' confidence, and wind them round my little finger.'

'I expect you can!' says the nurse, smiling.

'Of course I can!' says Roz. 'I'm terrific! But it doesn't fall within the usual job description of cook/ housekeeper, does it?'

'Well, you don't, come to that. Fall within the usual description, I mean. How do you come to be doing this?'

'Why shouldn't I?'

'Well, perhaps I'm being nosy. But, – lovely accent, expensive clothes . . .'

'Oh, I see. Well, you know how it is these days. My husband has decided he prefers a younger woman – something mint-new out of school – the house is being sold to divide between us, and suddenly I need somewhere to live and some way of earning money. I wasn't expecting it; a Cordon Bleu cookery course is the only qualification I ever bothered to get, and that was years ago. I wasn't thinking of a live-in job, really. Far too restricting. But this is so well-paid! I thought I'd stand it for a few days. I didn't know it would be a kind of morgue. That's why I skived off last night. I don't know how you stick it!'

'Ah,' says the nurse. 'Well, one gets attached to people, in my line. Have you clapped eyes on your clients, yet?'

'Only that glimpse we both got from the boxroom window. But their lunch is ready. I suppose I'd better go and look for them.'

As Alfie's car disappears under the arching lime trees of the avenue, Fleur turns to Dora, and hugs

44

her. They are both in tears. They seem to be unsteady on their feet, and they sway together, uncertain whether they are rushing to their room to cover their heads and lie crying, or whether they should collect themselves and return to their work.

'I was coming to look for you,' says a voice behind them. 'Your lunch is ready.'

'But who are you?' says Fleur, hastily wiping her eyes. She is looking at a woman a few years older than herself, standing in a butcher's apron in the doorway of the house. 'I'm Rosemary,' the woman says, 'but everyone calls me Roz. I'm the house-keeper. And I have strict instructions to look after you well. So won't you come in for lunch?'

They follow her. She leads them along the inter-connecting rooms of the Palladian front, chatting pleasantly, telling them how pleased she is to have got the job, and how she looks forward to living for a few weeks in this lovely house, and how good the nearest shops have proved, and how strange the kitchens, and then she opens a door disguised as a bookcase, of which Fleur on her initial exploration had not the slightest suspicion, and which leads into a snug little Gothic breakfast room with a wide bay window on to the garden, blue wallpaper rampant with curling white lilies, a bright little fire taking off the chill of disuse, and a table set with flowers and food. There are several salads in big bowls, a crusty quiche on a platter, a dish of cold salmon, a basket of hunks of brown and white bread, a cut-glass dish in which curls of butter are piled on crushed ice, and, completing the array, two places set with old silver flatware and white damask napkins.

'Sit down,' says Roz, 'and I'll bring you sorrel soup. I've been making it all morning, and it's perfect now.'

Her two distraught charges do sit down; but before the service lift has delivered the soup tureen Dora cries suddenly, 'I'm sorry, but I couldn't eat! I don't want anything . . . I . . .', and she jumps up, overturning her chair.

Whereupon Fleur too, tears coursing down her cheeks, says quietly, 'I'm afraid I . . . I couldn't eat anything, either.'

'Why you poor things, whatever is the matter?' asks Roz. 'Whatever has upset you?'

'We have just heard that our fiancés have gone away,' says Fleur, unsteadily.

'For months!' cries Dora.

And Roz laughs. 'Oh, is that all?' she says cheerfully. 'You had me worried for a moment, I thought it was something serious!'

Dora whitens, and says with sudden fury, 'How dare you mock me! People get murdered for less!'

'Ouch! I'm sorry; I didn't mean it unkindly,' says Roz. 'But you must eat. Believe me, a little sorrel soup will do wonders for you; a little cold salmon and you'll see it all in proportion.'

'I am choking,' says Dora, 'and the light is hurting my eyes. I must go and lie down alone.'

'Because your fellow has gone off for a while? He'll be back!'

'Yes, Dora,' says Fleur, shakily. 'We mustn't worry. They will be back!'

'But is there any doubt of it?' asks Roz. 'Wherever have they gone?'

'They've gone rock-climbing on St Kilda, counting birds, or something,' says Fleur. 'It sounds horribly dangerous.'

'Fun for them, though,' says Roz. 'Taste the soup. They'll be having the time of their lives, and you won't even taste the soup! You should be thinking how to have a good time while they're away.'

'Really,' says Fleur, shaking her head, 'without them no sort of good time is possible.'

'Oh, come. It's a last chance for a fling, to have some sort of fun with somebody else, as no doubt they will be doing. They'll be chasing local girls . . .'

'It's an uninhabited island,' says Dora.

'Well, it would take more than that to stop a man laying someone. I bet there are girls going with them on this climbing trip.'

'I don't know what sort of men you know, Roz,' says Fleur with dignity, 'but, honestly, William will be faithful to me whoever is with them on the trip. I know it.'

'But that's too much!' cries Roz. 'What do you take me for? These days you couldn't kid a baby with such rubbish. Men, faithful? Men, far from home with nobody to tell tales on them, chaste? They're all the same, you know – about as steady as the weather! They only want one thing, and when they get it they despise us. If you want real kindness or reliable affection, you want a woman friend every time, believe me, it's no good wanting a man to feel sympathy. They've had it their own way for centuries, and now at last women have woken up; correction, most women have. Not you two, it seems. You pay them in their own coin, you enjoy yourselves any way you want, that's my advice.'

And as the two young women both sweep out, she says ruefully, 'and it took me all morning to make a delicious lunch . . . ah well. But they'll be hungry later . . .'

At which point the phone rings, loud in the resonant marble hall. It sounds violently intrusive in the hush of the quiet house. Roz picks it up and finds herself talking to her employer. It is a long and detailed conversation.

They had emptied the bottle of champagne, and moved on to Anna's essay.

'It is a point of some irony,' she read, 'that the aspect of the *Cosi* story which above all seems incredible to a modern audience and prevents the story from being taken seriously is not the aspect of the story which attracted the disapproval and disbelief of earlier generations. The cynicism and immorality of the tale have been commented on repeatedly, but the sheer impossibility of anyone being taken in for a minute by a disguise worn by someone reasonably well known to them seems to have become apparent only in modern times. Perhaps this is the result of the greatly decreased importance in modern society of "dress" as offering important indicators about people, about their rank, at least; and an enhanced interest in the person as an individual, in all that makes each person unique and differentiates each judge from other judges, each farmer from other farmers, each beggar from other beggars.

'It has been remarked – by you, sir, last week – that the plays of Shakespeare are full of disguises, while escaping censure as silly, so it seems instructive to consider for purposes of comparison the role of disguises in Shakespeare, and I shall look in turn at *A Midsummer Night's Dream, As You Like It,* and *Twelfth Night.* In *A Midsummer Night's Dream* the multiple transformations undergone by the characters are brought about by magic, and illuminate the fantastical imagery of love. The image of the beloved in the mind of the lover can differ grotesquely from that image in the minds of everyone else, the most extreme example being Titania doting on Bottom, with or without an ass's head, which can only be the result of some enchantment. But Shakespeare surely means this as an analogy with the way in which, in common experience, it may be impossible to see what a person in love sees in the beloved, and love nearly always has the qualities of the absurd for any onlooker. The mix-up with the main four lovers is almost a mirror image of the theme in *Cosi*; but when they address their endearments to the wrong women the joke is on them, they are the victims, not the perpetrators, of deception. The reliance on magic to produce illusions, however, of which there is no element at all in *Cosi*, closely resembles the magical element in disguising the suspicious husband, with the help of an enchantress, or a goddess, or some such which is prominent in the earlier versions of the story.

'In *As You Like It* the disguise of Rosalind is transexual, and, since Shakespeare had to use boy actors, it had a piquancy in his day that it doesn't have in ours. But the disguise has a liberating effect on Rosalind, who can do and say disguised what she could not do and say *in propria persona*. It is possible that the men in *Cosi* are benefiting from this emancipation, doing in their disguises what they would not be allowed to do in an open way; but the girls are not disguised, and are locked firmly to responsibility for their conduct, whereas Ferrando and Guglielmo never admit responsibility for the Albanian gentlemen. This may be part of the reason why *Cosi* seems so unfair.'

Alfie groaned. 'There we go again! That word "unfair". Somehow I would not have expected from you, Anna, the self-flattering belief that those caught out in infamy have been treated unfairly. Thomas, I have realized, is hopelessly romantic, but a woman, after all, is endowed with superior sense.'

49

Anna looked up at him, thoughtfully. She had washed the fluorescent colours out of her butchered hair, which was standing in soft glossy spikes all over her head. Her shirt was buttoned up to the chin, and she looked no more like a punk than Bottom looked like Oberon. But she frowned at Alfie, and said, 'The conduct I was referring to is not the conduct of the men in the opera, but the conduct of the opera by the librettist. It seems to be playing with the dice loaded against the women. There's a lack of ironic distance between author and drama.'

'And isn't an author's opinion usually detectable in his work, young Anna? Why should Da Ponte not propagate his point of view like all the rest? Isn't the real problem here simply that you resist the message, and wish to believe it untrue?'

'Well, no, sir, that isn't . . .'

'Wishing to believe it untrue, you feel that the proof must be flawed; that . . .'

'No, sir. After all I am not the only person to react in this way. *Cosi* has a long history of . . .'

'Being objected to. There at least, you are right. Why should that be, do you think? What, lost for an answer? Where were we?'

'Twelfth Night,' said Thomas.

Anna bent over her notepad, and read: '*In Twelfth Night* we are once again presented with disguise which is without the element of magic, though it is buttressed with a brother and sister pair who look as alike as two peas, and with false beliefs about the death of the other which each of them entertains, and anyway most of those deceived, like the Duke who takes Viola for a young man, had never clapped eyes on the person in question undisguised. The comparison with *Cosi* which suggests itself is the manner in which disguises complicate and illuminate false and true love. Of course, the disguise

50

adopted by Viola in *Twelfth Night* is innocent; she does not trick herself out as a man in order to entrap Olivia, but as a protection for herself cast among strangers. Nevertheless, when she realizes what has come of it she repents:

> "Poor lady, she were better love a dream.
> Disguise, I see thou art a wickedness
> In which the pregnant enemy does much . . ."

'However, the broadest comparison with *Twelfth Night* is the most illuminating. The play is dream-like, full of far-fetched occurrences, mistakes of identity, romantic disguises, people in love at first sight. But the play does not disown love; rather it underwrites it. When all the characters are assembled at the end, and the disguises penetrated, each lover shall have what he desires, whereas the atmosphere of *Cosi* is not dreamlike at all. The opera presents feelings of love, but would have us understand that they are all false; protestations of fidelity are broken within the hour, and the new love is abandoned and disowned in its turn equally quickly. Since it is impossible to believe that the feelings of any of the four protagonists for their original partner can be at the end of the opera what they were at the beginning, one might almost say that in the opera nobody gets what they desire.'

'I realize you might be difficult to persuade,' said Alfie, 'that Da Ponte is a profounder writer than the great W.S. But I think that what emerges at the end of *Cosi*, is not correctly stated in your essay, Anna. At the end of *Cosi*, it seems to me, it appears that what everyone desires does not exist; that the paragons of virtue adored by the stupid young men at the opening have been shown to be moonshine. The lovers must accept the women for what they really are; the message is realism, not despair. Tolerance, not judgement. The message is not that nobody is to get what they want, but that everybody must want what they can have. And that's true, too. Isn't it?'

'If you say so, sir,' said Anna, coldly.

'Oh! OH!' cried Alfie. 'Hoity-toity! Not if I say so, young woman, but if you can persuade the examiners to give you high marks for saying anything else!'

And Thomas came to her rescue. 'If you pull rank on us, sir, it is hard to see how we can discuss anything freely.'

At which for a second the room froze; they were both afraid of what Thomas had said. Alfie was formidable, powerful; neither of them knew what happened if a student quarrelled with a tutor.

But Alfie just laughed. 'Quite right,' he said. 'And of course you are to say what you like, and learn from me if you can, only if you can . . . and clearly you have put a lot of thought and work into this essay, Anna, but I really can't see that disguises are any better than a side issue. They are necessary in *Cosi* because each sister has seen her sister's betrothed. But imagine, if you will, a similar experiment taking place today. The two girls need not be sisters, in which case, as long as they never catch sight of their own dear one wooing the other . . .'

'That sounds even more far-fetched than the opera,' said Thomas.

'Well, well,' said Alfie, 'things sometimes are fetched from far. There is nothing in such a proposal as extraordinary as an ancient university's procedures for teaching pupils, is there?'

'Shall I go on?' said Anna.

'You mean there is more? But the allotted time is almost over; I hear the Merton chimes, do I not? Spare me, my dear, spare me.' He got up, and held open the door for them to leave.

'But what shall we do for next week?' asked Thomas.

'You might repair the deficiencies in your knowledge of Shakespeare,' said Alfie, sighing. 'The play to compare with *Cosi* is *Love's Labour's Lost*, pre-eminently. I do quite see that even the title might have put you off; but love's labours always are lost, you know,' and he closed the door on them, the oak, and then the inner door, followed by the sound of the exaggerated iron key turning in the lock, and left them standing on the landing of the worn and time-bleached ancient stairs, fragrant with wax. And Anna in tears.

Whereas a girl might weep into her pillow in her room alone, unchecked for hours, two girls weeping in the same room are bound to check each other, and to resort to confidences. And of course, there will be consolation for each in the other's misery. Neither of them will think it dramatized, or over the top, to be in such distress over a temporary parting. Of course, each in her own heart knows her own pain to be sharper, because it arises from separation from someone whom she knows to be superior to the other's – indeed to any other's – loved one.

And Fleur is not so prostrated by grief that she cannot befriend Dora, put a sisterly arm round her, bring her a sponge wrung out in cold water to cool her burning face, and urge her gently to talk instead of weeping. Though what she hears amazes her.

'We were so lucky to find him,' Dora tells her.

'Who's "we"?'

'My family. My uncle found him.'

'You mean it was arranged for you?' Fleur exclaims. 'I thought all that went out with the flood.'

'It is usual, among my people.'

'An uncle found him, and you fell in love with him?'

'He is perfect for me,' says Dora, sighing.

'How can he be perfect if your uncle chose him?' Fleur is having trouble muting her sense of outrage.

'Western girls who choose for themselves are not always happy,' says Dora, gently.

'Well, no, but . . .'

'And I thought it would be hopeless to find a husband for me. I thought I would become an old maid.'

'How could you? You are so beautiful!' Fleur speaks as she finds, envying Dora's heavy black hair, glinting blue, the flawless smoothness of her skin, coloured like autumn honey, and most of all the slender build and grace of movement of her friend.

'But you see, I was brought up in England, and that would make me a bad wife for a boy from home. It would be hard to convince his family that I would not try on western ways.'

'Aren't there any boys brought up in England?'

'Not too many of my caste. And besides, my father is hoping that I will marry someone at home. He would like to have a daughter to visit there.'

'But what do you think?'

'I do not want to go to live in India. You have to do everything your mother-in-law tells you. And it would be hard for me to use my diploma, to work in a garden there. Home for me is here.'

'Tell me about Fernando.'

'He is very rich. I shall have a garden of my own.'

'But you don't love him for his money!'

'Of course not. He is very kind. He has been to school in England all his childhood, and he would like a modern wife. His mother is dead, and he is worried about his sister; she is still very young, and

54

she is looked after by very old-fashioned aunties. When we are married we will bring her to England, and show her a bit of modern life. I was quite sure he was the right one for me, even before we met.'

'Before?' Fleur is appalled. 'And when you did meet?'

'At once we liked each other.'

But Fleur is still baffled. 'But do you really, truly, love him?'

'I am longing for him day and night. I think I shall die from longing for him.'

And that certainly sounds convincing.

Dora, looking up red-eyed, but calm now, says, 'And how was it with you and William? Tell me about you.'

So Fleur embarks on her own story. She describes herself sitting on a flowery brink, on a sea-cliff, with her easel and paints, trying for the sunlit distance with its beguiling lighthouse, while the surf whispers clamorously below, and little clumps of spume ascending on the thermal up the cliff-face drift like thistledown over the flower-starry grasses. Walkers on the cliff path were passing by, and some of them stared at her work, and made assinine comments. Then a sudden fierce gust twitched the little canvas from its lodging, and spun it upwards, and when it fell it skated on the buffering air, and slid over the edge. And a young man appeared from nowhere, looked over the brink, said 'Don't worry,' and hitched a rope round a jut of rock, and lowered himself over the drop, after it. Recalling her terror makes her tremble even now; how it made her dizzy even to look down at him, and how he was walking himself down on the end of his rope, down, down, and reaching out, gently extracting her canvas from the giddily-perched gorse bush that had netted it. How scared she had been for him! He had brought it back to her smiling, and said, 'It's good.'

'Not good enough to risk life for!' she had said, still shaken.

'Depends on the life?' he had said, and, 'Mine would be improved no end if you would have a drink with me.'

She could hardly have refused. 'When?' she had said. 'Where?'

'Here and now,' he had said, and opening his rucksack he had produced a bottle of wine and a plastic beaker.

So they had talked till the strengthening wind had driven them off the clifftop, and then in the room Fleur had rented for the week. Thinking of all this she cannot help thinking of William suspended over fierce distant cliffs in far St Kilda, in operations even more terrifying – he had told her that climbing down for her picture was easy – and the thought brings tears to her eyes so that she would have been weeping again, had a cold little thought not struck her: though she had chosen William without benefit of uncle, entirely at her own will, entirely freely; though the crest of the cliff would be levelled to the beach by the airy winds sooner than her love for him would change or fade, though she had spent days and nights with him compared to Dora's three short chaperoned afternoons, yet she knows far less about him, either about his past, or what future he might offer, than Dora knows about Fernando.

Thomas found it unbearably painful to see Anna in distress. She clattered down the stairs faster than could have been safe, for surely it is hard to see clearly with tears springing freely to one's eyes, and spilling over?, and fled across the court so that he

56

had to run to catch up with her. He put a hand on her shoulder, and she turned to face him.

'Anna, what is the matter? I mean, don't be upset . . .'

'Oh, it isn't fair!' she wailed. 'Thomas, I spent hours and hours on that essay, and I really minded about it, and I dug up all sorts of stuff, and he didn't let me finish, he didn't even let me get to the best bit, so bloody patronizing and rude, saying "spare me," like that, and he let you read yours, – just because you're a man . . . I thought we'd stopped all that stupid prejudice, and it's good stuff, Thomas, it really is – I hate him – I shall go to my moral tutor and ask to be sent to someone else, the beast!'

'Oh no, Anna, don't do that!' said Thomas in alarm.

'Why not?' said Anna, sniffing and wiping her cheeks fiercely with the back of her hands.

'Because I'd . . .' His voice trailed away. If he told her he would miss her horribly what would she think he meant? He had loaded such commonplace nice remarks with a possible awful ambiguity. Indeed he had tripped himself into a minefield with her in every way. He never saw a girl more in need of a coffee, but if he offered her one, would she think he meant . . . ?

'Come for a coffee?' he tried. After all, he couldn't very well leave her in such a state, she must realize that.

'Where?' she said at once.

'Well, the Tackley?' He pointed vaguely through the college gate. He couldn't quite bring himself to say, 'Not in my room', in case she hadn't been thinking of last week. He cursed inwardly as he realized that he would never again be able to ask her to his room without sounding like a seducer.

'I can't go anywhere like this,' she said dejectedly.

'If there's one thing that looks terrible with red hair, it's red eyes . . . I do wish I didn't cry so easily. I'm always doing it, and I despise it so! Besides it makes me look awful.'

'Oh no, Anna,' he said, suppressing a desire to say, 'compared to what you did to your hair it's a bagatelle!' and putting his arms round her he said instead, 'Sorrow proud to be advanced so . . .' and kissed her tenderly on her salty lips. Then with an arm round her shoulder he led her through the gate past the grinning junior porter, and towards the nearest coffee shop.

A little later, listening to her lamenting again the waste of essay, while the rumbling traffic up the High Street put a tension pattern on the surface of his creamy white coffee, and made the cup and saucer sing together softly, and agreeing – for he did agree – that setting an essay and then being unwilling to listen to the result was abominable conduct, Thomas said, 'Anna, would it help at all if you read the rest of it to me? I mean, there's no reason why you should care what I think, but if you want to . . .'

'But wouldn't you be bored stiff?'

'No, I wouldn't.' Longer with you!, he thought, but he said only, 'This is the most interesting subject I have worked on so far.'

'You see, I looked up Da Ponte, and he was incredibly disreputable. Quite extreme. And there was something that made me think, whatever we think about disguises, they may have seemed perfectly plausible to him.'

'Let's go somewhere quiet, and you can tell me all.'

Somewhere quiet, he decided, had to be out of doors. He still choked at the thought of his room, and suggesting hers, he saw at once, was no better. But it was a beautiful day. The summer was lingering into a golden autumn, unwilling to leave Oxford, and there were still punts in the water – they could take a punt. Just in time he stopped himself suggesting it, remembering the gently heaving entwined and prostrate forms one glimpsed in punts moored against the flowery banks behind the half screening bead-curtains of the willow fronds . . . his mind pulsated with images of copulation. Should he perhaps simply tell her that he had no intention . . . I will never fuck you again, Anna . . . God, no! For one thing, he could not bear the thought of a life in which he never again fucked Anna. I will never fuck you again, Anna, uninvited? But that might sound like fishing for an invitation. He stole a sideways glance at her, striding along beside him, her tears dry on her cheeks. Her eyes were swollen-lidded, and the tears had stuck the soft faint downiness of her cheeks flat to her skin. She had, for the moment, an appearance of starlet sensuality. He looked away again, hastily, and led her into the meadow.

They found a sunlit bench, against the battered mellow stonework of the old city wall, looking at the random incursions of thistle and goldenrod in the uncut grass. Far too public for her to think he meant anything, and quiet, apart from the small ecstasies of a thousand birds. He spread his coat out on the bench for her to sit on, in case it felt damp, and then sat down beside her chastely to hear about the history of an Italian libertine, two centuries ago.

'Tell me about the disreputability,' he said. 'I'm looking forward to that.'

'Well, he was a sort of unfrocked priest. To start with he was a Jew, and then he converted, and then he just ran off to Venice and fell into evil ways.'

'Hold it; a little more detail, please.'

'He was born a Jew. Then his mother died, and his father wanted to marry a Christian lady. So the father had to become a Christian, the whole family were baptized, and the bishop gave the little boys his own name – Da Ponte – and took them under his wing. He saw to their education by sending them to a seminary. Lorenzo's brother turned into a solid, good priest, who always did what he could for his brother; Lorenzo turned into a kind of poetry-writing Casanova.'

'But he did get ordained?'

'Yes, he did. It didn't seem to stop him having mistresses, and keeping low company, gambling and writing political lampoons that got him into trouble. As far as I can see it never meant a thing. He seems to have expressed bitter regret at having let it happen.'

'But it didn't inhibit him?'

'No. His entire youth seems to have been one amorous adventure after another, many of them involving scandal.'

'So he isn't really a person whose moral advice would have much authority?'

'Certainly not, if you would like to take moral advice from a virtuous person. Of course, if you want advice about love from someone with a lot of experience . . .'

'Well, a person with a lot of experience wouldn't necessarily know much about faithful love, would they?' said Thomas. 'You obviously can't get expert in that by whoring around.'

'Hmm. Anyway, Da Ponte wouldn't have agreed with my description of him. He wrote his memoirs later in life, and he offers the most impudent self-defence. Just listen to this: *"From the moment when I first fell in love at the age of eighteen, until the forty-second year of my life, when I took a companion for the remainder of it, I have never said to a woman 'I love you' without knowing I could love her*

60

without any breach of honour. Often my intentions, my glances and even compliments paid out of common civility were taken as declarations of love, but my mouth never sinned, and never without the consent of heart and reason did I try through vanity or whim to awaken in an innocent or credulous breast a passion which could only end in tears and remorse . . ." and that, mind you, is what he has to say for himself on being forbidden to cross the threshold of a household in which he has been courting a mother and two daughters, and has all three in love with him!'

'Anna, that is really interesting!' said Thomas. 'Can I copy that bit into my notes?'

'Well, of course, if you want. But it isn't the most interesting bit.'

'Tell me what the most interesting bit is.'

'It's about Venice. I'll read it to you, it's full of quotes.' She turns the leaves of her essay, and clears her throat and sits straight, so that he has for a moment a sense of decorum between them, as if he were really her tutor. Then she resumes reading.

'Da Ponte spent years of his youth in Venice, a city which revelled in an unusually glamorous and unconstrained society. Women were free to stroll the streets, and drink in coffee houses, and converse with strangers. A great carnival took place there, to which even kings and queens were drawn, including that very Joseph II for whom *Cosi* was written; he went twice, and he went incognito. The city had dozens upon dozens of open sunny piazzas, warm late into the lilac evenings, and lit by lamplight all night long, with no horses or traffic pouring through them, which were used like the rooms of a palace by all the citizens, rich and poor mingling freely and leading their lives in the streets as though at home, enjoying alike the dazzling beauty of the façades, and on every possible occasion processing and dancing in the streets. The Venetians loved music; vagrant musicians performed on every corner, and "if two of the common people walk together arm in arm they are always singing, and seem to converse in song; if there is company on the water it is the same; a mere melody unaccompanied by a second voice is not to be heard in this city . . ." The city was full of wine shops and coffee shops – there was even one called the *"Caffè de'letterati"* where intellectuals and poets gathered – of bookshops, gambling dens and brothels . . . doesn't it sound wonderful, Thomas?'

He laughed. 'All that, and beauty too! Luscious reflections in the dark canals, gondolas, marble, bronze, a thousand years expanding cloudy wings! No wonder it went to your man's head.'

'Yes, but there's an even more pointed point coming up. Listen to this . . . Lamartine called Venice a permanent masked ball: "masks were universally worn, and this gave wearers a licence that would otherwise have been impossible. It also led to a particularly classless society. Nobleman and beggar, artisan and poet, gondolier and visiting royalty mingled under the clear winter sky, protected by their masks."'

'Wow!' said Thomas. 'Where are you getting all this, Anna?'

'It's in a stunning book about Da Ponte by Sheila Hodges. There's more. A fantastic thing seems to have happened to Da Ponte. He was sitting in the *Caffè de'letterati*, when a gondolier appeared and tugged his sleeve. He thought his mistress had sent for him, as she often did, so he got into the gondola with a masked lady, and then it appeared that she had mistaken him for her lover, as he had mistaken her for his mistress!'

'So, however hard it is to believe that you could be disguised from your lover, this is something that had actually happened to Da Ponte; is that what you're saying?'

'Well, it's the other way round, isn't it? They didn't fail to recognize the right person in disguise; they recognized the wrong person.'

'Is that very different?'

'It might be. But what makes the real difference, don't you think, is masks. Da Ponte had experienced the effect of masks; perhaps he didn't realize how silly it was to think of disguises working without masks.'

'If your disguise covers your face, then it might work, you think?' says Thomas. He is baffled slightly by her excitement. Somehow, however kind he feels, however pretty the picture of Venice she is drawing for him, he can't get as concerned about disguises as she is. 'Who was she really?' he asks.

'Who was who?'

'The lady in the gondola.'

'A runaway nun, who had been forced into a convent because she wouldn't marry an old and ugly husband. She ran away to Venice because where everyone went masked it was easier to hide. She offered gold and jewels to Da Ponte to take her under his wing, but he hesitated, and she got captured and put back in the convent.'

'He does seem to have had a dramatic sort of life.'

'It goes on, and on. Blackmail, pretended alchemy, one love affair after another, persecution, exile . . . then amazing success, writing libretti for one composer after another, hobnobbing with emperors . . .'

'And yet he would be wholly forgotten now, nameless and unimportant, if he hadn't happened to meet Mozart. For all his wickedness and glamour he's only a walk-on part in another man's life. It's pathetic, really.'

'No, you underestimate him. He was as tough as old shoe leather; he started a new life over and over again, as often as he was ruined. And you'll never guess how he finished up – as a professor of Italian in Columbia University in New York, and a moving spirit in founding the New York Opera House!'

'I take it back. Only Anna, tell me – I'm obviously being slow – explain to me, what is the heart of all this, in your view?'

'I've been explaining all afternoon!'

And it was getting late. The shadows on the meadow were gently creeping towards them, reading tea-time on to the Broadwalk. They both had other things to do.

'Put it in a nutshell,' he suggested.

'Well, the disguise motif in *Cosi* seems pretty fatuous at first sight,' she said. 'If it's just a stage convention, then it's too stagy, it turns the whole thing into nothing but farce. And it isn't as if we were told it was magic, or anything to sugar the pill, to help us believe it. But in the light of Da Ponte's amazing life it is possible that he himself thought the disguises plausible, and intended them to provoke not incredulity, but thought. As well as laughter, of course.'

'OK. So if we do accept them, and are provoked to thought – what thought, exactly?'

'You perceive that disguises are a licence – like the Lord of Misrule, or the day of the Boy Bishop, or something. Think of the effect alleged on Venetian society, open and free, with liberty for women, with mixing of rich and poor, "*which would not otherwise have been possible*". You escape responsibility completely for what you do and say, – it is not tracked back to your real self at all. Thomas, don't you see? – don't think of disguise as concealing you

64

from others – it conceals you from yourself. If you can wear one mask you can wear dozens, you can be anyone, anything, and all that you say or do while masked can be disowned!'

At that Thomas flinched as though she had struck him. He had forgotten that he was standing in for Alfie, hearing her essay. He had forgotten that she was reading what she had written as a student. He heard her disown utterly what she had done in black leather, with her hair blazing pink and green. It had nothing to do with her true self, and only for that reason had it been possible. He was surprised that he was not screaming, as he would have been screaming had he suddenly been burnt or mangled physically, but the hurt was silent, for he heard only birdsong.

And she mistook the agony on his face for pronounced disagreement, and said eagerly, 'Thomas, you must see, you must. This is what makes *Cosi* seem so bitterly unfair, such an outrage; the men are at liberty to be as libertine as they like, and it's never brought home to them; they never accept the least responsibility for what those Albanians are up to, whereas the girls are held to account, and blamed for every little sigh, every single unguarded word! What's so unfair is just that the men are disguised, and those poor girls are not!'

Since she knows that Dora cannot have slept – how could distressed love sleep? – Fleur does not ask her how the night went. Refreshed herself, realizing that she herself has slept sweetly all night after the first half-hour, she does not wish to be asked in return. A bright morning shines through the rigged-up curtain with which they have covered their window, and somehow the weight of grief feels less crushing in the early light. And breakfast too will be embarrassing. Fleur is ravenous; skipping both lunch and supper yesterday had already taken romantic aversion to food much further than a healthy young woman can bear; if Dora doesn't eat breakfast, and so demonstrates a deeper and more sincere attachment to Fernando than she can herself demonstrate to William, what shall she do? 'If I don't eat,' she tells herself, 'I'll be reduced to sneaking out for bars of chocolate long before lunch-time.'

Increasing her hunger pangs, a faint but eloquent aroma of frying bacon meets them half way down the stairs.

'Goodness, am I hungry!' says Dora.

'So am I!' says Fleur, hugging her in pure relief.

And they tuck in, tackling porridge with syrup, and bacon and eggs, and a mountain of toast with Marmite, and cup after cup of coffee, and Fleur feels better and better, so that eventually she says, not realizing that Roz has appeared with a second pot of coffee, and is standing just behind her chair, 'Isn't it rather disgraceful to be so cheered by food?'

'Human, certainly,' says Roz.

'Work will take our minds off our sorrow,' says Dora primly, 'and we can't work on empty stomachs.'

'You are right, of course,' says Fleur. Was she? Was anything supposed to take your mind off it? 'I must go and get into working clothes,' she adds. 'Cleaning is dirty work, if you see what I mean.'

'Me too,' says Dora. 'I'll have to cover up. There's a swarm in a tree that I want to prune, and I must move it first.'

So while Fleur climbs into a khaki boilersuit, and ties a red cotton scarf round her head, pushing every stray wisp of hair underneath it, Dora is putting on a shiny grey jumpsuit with elasticated wrists and neck, and adding gloves and a wide-brimmed hat swathed in yards of green netting. Then they part, Dora for the enclosed and secretive topiary garden, and Fleur for the music room, where, now she no longer needs to linger by the door in hope of William, she has decided to begin.

The music room is part of the Palladian building. It has bas-relief columns, dividing the walls into *trompe l'oeil* colonnade, and two fine Ionic pillars framing the apsidal dais at one end. A sheeted grand piano occupies this stage, and a pile of chairs stand in a corner. On the south wall, the colonnade frames large windows, finely proportioned, looking over the terracing to the driveway and the front approach to the house. On the north wall the space between the columns has been painted with scenes in period dress. The paintings are not old, though until she has cleaned them a little Fleur cannot precisely date them. They have that sketchy execution that suggests the twenties. And they are absolutely filthy, coated with yellow-brown grime, which will smell, Fleur guesses, of nicotine. A billiard cue lying in a corner suggests that the room has been used as a games room, a smoking room, as much as for music. But the paintings – unless they are by a yet-to-be-discovered twentieth-century genius – cannot be as valuable as many in the house, and there is room for Fleur's barrage of bottles, sponges, gels, brushes and rags. And good light. She has decided to get her hand in by starting with these.

The first scene shows two young women in long dresses, on a balcony overlooking the sea, the arm of the taller curled lightly round the waist of the other. They are waving improbably long and sinuous handkerchiefs. Fleur coats a small area of the bottom right-hand corner with a viscous mix that will hold the cleaning chemicals against the dirt, and pouring a bowl of distilled water, picks up a clean sponge.

Meanwhile, in the kitchen, Roz, presented with William and Ferdy, stares impudently at them, says, 'I wouldn't fancy either of you, myself!' and gives them directions through the maze of house and garden.

Shortly, then, William finds himself in a ruined garden, between high walls of yew, approaching what looks like a large-headed robot on a ladder. His path towards it is loomed over left and right by blurred mythological figures of sinister import, like the 'things' which lurked in the garden nightmares of childhood. The hum of insects which he associates vaguely with gardens, and takes no notice of, is warming up as he gets nearer, until by the time he is near enough to say, 'Can I help?' he seems to be the subject of personal bombardment, as by aliens in a video game.

'Keep well back!' says the robot. She – for a she it must be – is holding a cardboard box in one hand, and a gadget in the other which puffs clouds of smoke at her adversaries, and thus she has no hand left free for holding on to the ladder. She is covered with bees, crawling all over her from head to foot, and colliding with the clouds of net that cover her head. In front of her a humming, pullulating globe of bees swells like a golden carbuncle on a branch.

'You do seem to need help,' says William, thinking about belting and running.

'Well . . . do you know about bees?' says the voice from the faceless net.

'Not a thing. I'm just the new gardener.'

'Go and get yourself a veil. There's a spare one on the wheelbarrow just over there.'

He finds it lying on top of mysterious things, frames holding embossed golden sheeting, white boxes without bottoms or tops, round discs like alabaster, but with one surface poured, like fudge. Everything, the veil included, reeks with a pungent sweetness. When he comes back with it she says crossly 'Put it on, then!' He finds himself peering through the cascades of netting hanging from the brim of the hat.

'Tuck it in,' she says in that tone of saintly patience that sings with scorn. He has got several bees inside it, but they seem content to crawl on his neck, and make vain attempts to fly away through the net. A terrible thought strikes him that should Fleur by any awful chance catch glimpses of him from the house while he is doing this – Alfie swore the garden could not be seen from the windows, but who would trust Alfie? – he might not merely be recognized, but be recognized looking stupid. A bee gets up speed beside his right ear, trying again to crash through the net.

'Hold this,' his taskmaster is saying. She is leaning down, handing him the box. He grabs the ladder with one hand, and the box with the other. 'Now hold it flat and steady, right under the swarm. Don't move, and don't flinch; they don't like the smell of fear. And whatever you do, don't drop it. Right?'

Rigid with fright, he nods, dumbly. It hadn't occurred to him when he undertook this bet, that Ferdy might be in love with a monster!

'Ready?' she calls, and sharply shakes the branch. In a dry rustling cascade the bees pour into the box, weighing it suddenly, so that he staggers, and tenses his arms. His tormentor skips lightly down the ladder, and puffs clouds of smoke at them, making him cough. She whips a lid on to the box, and says 'Got them!'

He blinks. The heat under the net is choking him, let alone the smoke. And his arms are hurting – badly. Looking down he sees that the net had been lying across his naked forearms, close to his skin, and several bees who had missed the box and landed on him, have stung him through it.

'Don't move!' she says, taking the roaring box, and setting it down. He is desperate to wriggle free of the net, to brush the bees off his flesh, but she seizes his hands, and holds hard. 'Wait,' she says. 'Don't brush them off. You'll kill them if you do.'

'Kill *them*?' he cries. 'What about me?'

'Better for you, too,' she says. 'Wait. Watch.'

So they stand hand in hand – she has a strong, steady grip through her sting-proof gloves, – and he watches the bees walking on him in circles, tugging their tethered abdomens. Round, and round . . . one frees itself, and flies off, then another . . . but it takes more time than he can endure. He jerks his head, and the net is twitched away from his left arm, freeing him instantly, leaving five stings behind.

'Look,' says Dora, holding his hand, and stretching his arm. 'Do you see those little sacs? Those are the toxin sacs. You brush them off, the sacs rip out of their bodies, and the sacs contract and pump the stuff into you. If you wait they extract the sting, and fly off with the poison unused. I can promise you now your left arm will hurt more than your right.'

'Thank you!' he says bitterly. 'And to think how I longed to get this job!'

'I am sorry you were stung,' she says. 'You wanted this job specially?' She has picked up the box of bees, and is carrying it along the path, so that he has to walk with her to keep talking.

'I wanted to work with you,' he says. 'You must be the most beautiful gardener since Eve!'

Dora laughs. 'You have never seen me except in a bee veil!' she says.

'The other night, in the pub. You were eating supper with some other girl. I couldn't take my eyes off you. I haven't been able to sleep for thinking of you.'

Dora stops laughing. 'Stop that at once,' she says. 'It's perfectly absurd, and I won't have it. I am engaged, and I have no intention of listening to such talk.'

'Be kind,' he says. 'Just let me work near you. Just let me talk to you.'

'But not talk like that. Leave me alone.'

'But what's wrong with me?' he asks her, pulling off the swathes of netting from his head, and emerging tousled in full view. 'I'm crazy, I admit, but I'm good fun; and I am handsome, aren't I? Look at me, dearest, do! You won't find brighter eyes, a straighter nose, a better smile . . .' He is starting to laugh.

But her outrage saves him. 'Really it isn't funny!' she yells at him. 'And if you don't take yourself off and work in another part of the garden I shall get you dismissed.'

That's over the top, he thinks. Why is she as angry as that? He says, 'The owner took me on specially.' His arms are hurting badly, he can't concentrate on his act. 'He thought you would like me. My instructions are to assist you at all times. That means being in the same part of the garden.'

Dora has reached a gate into an orchard, still within sight of the tree where the swarm was hanging. Here she has spread a groundsheet, and laid out four bricks. Carefully, she upends the box on top of the bricks, and slides the lid away from under it. There is a gap between box and groundsheet for the stragglers to come in.

'And how can I assist you without telling you how beautiful . . .'

She stands erect. Her eyes would be burning with rage could he see them, but the dark net still shades

71

her utterly from view. 'Piss off out of here, before I shake the bees out of the box!' she says. A thing which she has no intention of doing.

And at that he takes to his heels immediately. 'Good riddance!' she says, wheeling the barrow through into the orchard, and stacking up the frames and supers, the carefully prefabricated new home for the bees, full of undrawn combs stamped with blueprint honeycomb, 'What impudence!'

One is supposed to talk to bees. 'You must not imagine,' she tells her newcomers, walking back past the purring inverted box, 'that things will carry on like that. I am a respectable person, and engaged to dearest Ferdy, and I have no intention of standing any nonsense from anyone. You need have no fear of that.'

Though whether bees prefer to live with chaste and faithful people must be open to speculation, she reflects, going back through the orchard with the smell of smoke lingering about her veil, their sexual practices being unlike ours, though even more violent with redundant males.

Under Fleur's careful swabbing a stretch of the balcony floor is coming up bright and clear. The two girls in the painting are not standing, as at first appeared, on a brown wooden floor, but on a patterned marble mosaic, littered with fallen petals from flowers somewhere else in the picture. The smaller girl is barefoot – here appearing through the murk is the green velvet slipper she has cast off, with a yellow ribbon curling prettily from the heel. Fleur begins to work with broader strokes, and uncovers the thickly folded layers of a petticoat showing under the hem of the girl's white dress. The naked foot beneath the hem is arched, toes flat, heel lifted off the floor, as the painted girl stands on tiptoe, straining to see.

'I have come to help you,' says a voice.

Looking up, Fleur sees a swarthy young man, immaculately dressed, standing in front of her.

'Really?' she says. 'Are you trained?'

'Not formally, I'm afraid. But I have worked on murals.'

'Wherever did they let you work untrained?' she asks.

'Not in England,' he says. He is smiling at her; why? she wonders. 'But my uncle the Maharaja has a summer palace.'

'All right,' she says briskly. 'I'll give you a try. There's enough to be done. For a start go and ask Roz to find you some overalls, and find and bring a ladder.'

While he is gone she inwardly tells herself off for cheek, asking about his training, her own being so very newly complete. She has not cleaned more than a dozen or so pictures herself, in spite of her gold medal diploma, though of course her training was not limited to cleaning pictures. A straw hat, held against the billowing muslin of the girl's dress, and trimmed with yellow roses and yellow ribbons, the presence of which was perfectly unsuspected, is emerging now under the deft strokes of her sponge. But she is running low on the mix of cleaning fluids suspended in a gel of starch, with which she thickly plasters the surface of the painting, leaving it to soften the dirt for a while, before cleaning it off with distilled water on clean rags. Going to her box of bottles to mix another brew, slightly stronger, of the acetates that give the gel its bite, and finding she has no clean container, she tips her drinking water into the slop bucket, and carefully measures into the empty glass the brew of chemicals that she uses. She

73

is very lucky, she reflects as she resumes her work, to be here, doing this. It was all just odd coincidence. The owner had seen the announcement of her engagement in *The Times*, and written to ask if she was the same person as the one of whom he had heard such good reports as a restorer, and if she was by any chance free for a few weeks in the summer. She had been promised an assistant, and the newcomer must be he.

He reappears, by and by, carrying ladders, and wearing a blue apron. He has taken off his linen jacket, and rolled up his shirt sleeves. Together they slot the ladders together to make a working platform three feet off the floor. Then she mounts to the bosoms and shoulders of her girls, and leaves him cleaning the other side of the picture at the bottom, working across the floor. If he does any damage there it will not be hard to patch.

'What a privilege!' he remarks by and by.

'To scrub a floor?' she says, amused.

'To work at the feet of a beautiful woman.'

'Only one?' she stares at the linked pair in front of her. Seconds later the meaning of the singular remark strikes her. She stops working, hand poised, and stares at him.

'Only for you did I take the job,' he says. 'Only to be near you. I don't need the work. I am rich. I will show you a good time.'

'Don't be ridiculous,' she says. 'Shut up and get on.'

'Be kind to me,' he says. 'Someone as beautiful as you ought to be kind. You are a public hazard. People are bound to be in love with you.'

'Dressed in this?' she says. 'You are out of your tiny mind!'

'When you were painting in Syon Park,' he says, 'you did not see me, but I was watching you. The image of the girl painting has haunted my dreams.

And then, the other night, I saw you again, when you ate in the pub with your friend. When I found out you were working here I was overjoyed.'

'I assume you are joking,' says Fleur stiffly. 'The joke is not in very good taste. Let me tell you that I am engaged, and not available to be courted, in fun or otherwise.'

'Why, what harm would it do?' he says, smiling up at her. 'You will leave me severely disillusioned. I always thought that discovering herself to be adored by a stranger was more pleasing than gold and rubies to a woman . . . and here I am opening treasure chests to you . . . where is your fiancé?'

'On St Kilda,' she says concentrating closely on the pretty blond curls round the shell-pink ear of the shorter girl.

'More fool he. If you were mine I would not leave you alone for a minute. Will you come out with me tonight?'

'No. Certainly not.' Though she cannot stop herself thinking that had she not been engaged . . . there is laughter in his eyes, and a twitch of amusement at the corners of his mouth. She can believe he would show her a good time.

'Don't be cruel, my dear,' he says. 'What harm could it possibly do?'

'Look, if you are going to pester me,' she says, fiercely, 'I shall have to ask the owner to find me another assistant.'

'Ah, but I'm not just an employee, you know,' he says. 'I'm the owner's friend. I won't be that easy to get rid of. Why not give in, and say you'll come out for a drink? Don't you think your employer's friends are entitled to a little courtesy?'

'Yes. But they're not entitled to pester. Why didn't you just invite me out for a drink? Now I know it isn't just an idle invitation, I can't accept it.'

'You could. You could forget all about him, and run off with the one who loves you most. I do.'

'You are outrageous!' she says.

'Hey, look at this!' he answers, and she frowns down, expecting a trick, only to see that he has uncovered a bright square patch on the area of marble floor emerging under his sponge. She climbs down at once, and comes to stare at it.

'I don't know what that is,' she says. 'Go easy. That's it, gently, gently . . . it might be a repair. If so we don't want to lay it naked . . . wait . . . go on a bit . . .' Their heads are close together as they peer intently at the surface of the paint.

'It's a buckle!' he says in a minute. 'A shoe buckle, don't you think?'

'Whose shoe? Is there someone else in this picture?'

'Hiding under all this dirt? Shall we see?' he says, and both together dipping their brushes and sponges, they begin to work closely side by side, uncovering a black shoe with a silver buckle, then the other shoe, then a pair of black-stockinged calves, and velvet knee-breeches; there is no doubt about it. The two sunlit girls, waving on their balcony, are not alone. Behind them, in the shadows, a man is standing, looking on.

What Anna had said about the exculpating force of disguises was perfectly true, and like a theme underlying variations would apply, *mutatis mutandis*, the other way about. Thomas, waking next morning, still smarting inwardly, gave it his gloomy attention. What she had done transmogrified into the punk rocker was not to be referred back to her everyday self; but what he had done he had done barefaced, and he could not disown it. Not that he wanted to disown it exactly – yes he did! For ever and ever his relationship with Anna would contain it. The other night he had overheard some fellow in the common room telling a story: – how he had seen this remarkably pretty girl painting on a clifftop, and how the picture had blown away, and he had done a nifty bit of climbing and brought it back to her, and got into conversation . . . whereas the story of Thomas's love, if he ever had the effrontery to tell it, would go: 'and the very first time I was ever alone with her I seized her, and tore off her clothes, and half carried, half dragged her to bed . . .' It was his own shame and chagrin that made Thomas sympathize so readily with Fiordiligi and Dorabella. The whole thing was bitterly unfair. It was also getting out of hand. He went through the frosty morning streets for a newspaper to read over breakfast in hall, to take his mind off his woes.

It would not have been wholly successful, containing as it did a long article called 'All Men are Rapists', but he was joined by friends, demanding a look at the sports pages, who removed the paper and shared it among themselves. Thomas put up no resistance.

'Are you all right, Thomas, old thing?' Peter enquired. 'You don't seem yourself this morning.'

And that was it, in a nutshell. When was Thomas himself? The dreadful possibility that was keeping him squirming was that his true self was the greedy beast that had assaulted Anna. On the other hand it was already apparent that the beast appeared only when she was disguised; he behaved himself much better when she was wearing her ordinary clothes. In fact the more he thought about it, he realized, with a welcome lift in his naturally buoyant self-esteem, the more he saw that the disguise had in fact, deceived, tempted, liberated both of them; – since he really didn't react like that to her ordinary incarnation, the effect had not been confined to the person who actually wore the kit, and the unfairness quotient was not as unbalanced as all that.

'Disguise, I see thou art a wickedness!' he said to Peter, who replied, 'Go and see Matron. I would if I was feeling funny, and burbling like that!'

Thomas, however, was feeling better. He bounced back up the staircase to his own room, and found Anna sitting in his armchair.

'Oh,' he said. 'Hullo. I, er . . .'

'Thomas, I'm sorry; you'll be sick of the sight of me.'

'No, I, er . . .'

'But I need to talk to you. Please.'

'I'll put some coffee on,' said Thomas, nervously cataloguing to himself what she was wearing. Navy skirt, grey silky blouse open at the neck – not too far – thin strand of silver chain round her neck, dark stockings – left one laddered – plain pumps, nothing to scare him except her russet hair, standing in stooks like a scythed cornfield. That was going to take years to grow out.

'I'm going bananas,' she said. 'I simply can't get him out of my mind. Every time I close my eyes, there he is in the shadows, leering at me.'

'I take it you mean Mr Lightdown?'

'Yes! Him.'

'And he's getting on your wick? You'll have to have black, I'm afraid.'

'You know how he keeps making those funny remarks?'

'Which in particular?'

'Oh, you know. Like when I said the disguises

78

were at the heart of it, and he said, no they weren't – don't you remember? – he said, "I've thought of a way round that" – something like that.'

'So he did.'

'Well, what do you think he meant by it?'

'Anna, I haven't a clue. He's crazy; everyone knows that.'

'Yes, but Thomas, last night, when I was trying to get to sleep, I couldn't get it out of my mind – I suddenly thought, what if he's doing it again?'

'I don't get it.'

'Well, I know it sounds loopy, impossible, but it's just that he's so horrible – what if he's trying it again? What if he's bet somebody, just like in the opera, that their lovers will . . . could he, do you think? I'm imagining it, aren't I?' When Thomas didn't answer she went on, 'It would make sense of those remarks he makes . . . don't laugh, Thomas!'

But Thomas wasn't laughing, he was thinking.

'He does have an absolutely dire reputation round here,' he said.

'What sort of reputation?'

'For choosing people, and manipulating them. He takes them over. They say if he takes you up you're made for life – unless you quarrel with him. He knows all sorts of people, can drop a word in the right ear for you when you want a job, that sort of thing.'

'All right, so is he using his influence, to try out the *Cosi* theorem again, in real life?'

'No, Anna, he can't be. He's just a poor old sod who likes to talk big, drop names, sound mysterious.'

'Is he rich?'

'Very. He paid for the work on the college clock himself.'

'So he could afford to make huge bets?'

'But, Anna, who would take them? Look, if your theory is right, that means there are two flesh-and-blood real men who are prepared to allow their partners to be tested, who are prepared to go off at someone else's bidding and pay court to someone they are not in love with.'

'It has been known for men to seduce women they are not in love with.'

And what could he say? 'I never would'? But what would that prove, apart from leaving him naked in her sight? He could say, 'I can't believe it,' but of course, in one way he could, she was quite right, it happened all the time.

'It would be so vile!' he said. 'So contemptible of everybody concerned.'

'But we know what he thinks of that. When you pointed out the vileness he called it shooting the messenger. And he isn't indifferent, Thomas, he isn't objective. He argues about it as though he really needed it to be true that everyone is always fickle.'

'All right. So suppose for a moment he is capable of making the bet, and someone is fool or knave enough to take it . . .'

'But they don't think they're knavish, Thomas. They are hard up, and they are sure they are going to win. They don't see much harm in it.'

'All right then, they are without true feeling, crass sort of oafs, and . . .'

'And hard up. It's interesting, isn't it? that the bribe that your early versions offered to the women has not disappeared from the story, but moved. Now it is applied to the men.'

'And they ought to know better. Doing something for money that you wouldn't dream of doing otherwise is slippery stuff, after all. So, Anna, suppose, just suppose, that you are right. Lightdown's few funny remarks indicate that he is experimenting with other people's happiness, just as you suggest. What could we do about it?'

'Stop him,' she said.

'Go easy,' says Fleur. 'If you try to work fast you'll get a streaky effect.'

Their excitement at uncovering the unsuspected hidden figure is as great as if they could apprehend him, challenge him as an intruder. They are working close together, close enough to hear each other's breathing, to inhale the faint aroma of each other's skin. Quite quickly they have fallen into step with each other, so that as one reaches backwards to dip a sponge the other leans out of the way; a sort of slow, working dance is being performed. And of course, the work is going much faster with two. Fleur is just beginning to think the assistant might be a good thing, when he says, 'It's thirsty work, this.' He leans backwards, and picks up something from the work trolley. A sudden smell of acetate, as though he spilled something, and a choking sound are quickly followed by the crash of glass breaking on the marble floor.

So Fleur, looking round a second too late to see what really happened is confronted by her assistant lying gasping and twitching on the floor. The drinking glass in which she had mixed the acetate is scattered in glittering fragments across the marble from his outflung right hand. Little plosive choking sounds stutter from his throat.

Fleur runs. Across the music room and down the Palladian gallery, past the sweeping stairs, towards the breakfast room, and the steps to the kitchens. She is screaming as she goes, yelling, 'Roz! Help, Roz!' and running so fast that she collides with Roz full tilt at the breakfast room door. Then they are both running, back to the music room.

'Is he breathing?' demands Roz. Falling to her knees beside the stranger, Fleur leans close to his face.

'Yes. Not deeply.'

'We should turn him over, and flex his arm and leg,' says Roz.

'Shouldn't we make him vomit? Salty water to drink?'

'No, I believe not. We fetch help, and we keep him warm. And if he stops breathing we administer the kiss of life. Can you do that? Did you ever learn it?'

'At school,' Fleur says. 'I've never done it.' She is trembling slightly, as though the disaster had been to herself. But the poor young man is also trembling; she is close enough to see the shivering of his lower lip.

'We need a blanket,' she says, looking up at Roz.

'I'll get something,' says Roz. It is probably half a mile to the nearest bedroom or linen cupboard in this barn of a house, but Roz is back almost at once with a fine embroidered curtain she has simply pulled off a pole. They roll up one edge of it, shoving the glass splinters out of the way across the floor with the sides of their shoes, and laying it beside the young man's supine form; they lift him between them, turning him over on to a doubled thickness of the curtain, and covering him with the rest. Fleur rolls up an edge to ease under his head.

'Don't take your eyes off him for a minute!' says Roz. 'If he stops breathing, do something! I'll go and phone a doctor. What did he drink, do you reckon? They'll want to know.'

'A cocktail of solvents, mostly acetate . . . I can't see if he's breathing or not!'

'Get down there, and stay close enough to be sure

you can see!' orders Roz, speeding off towards the nearest phone.

Fleur crouches down beside the casualty, and when that both freezes her knees on the cold marble, and doesn't really get her near enough to be quite sure, she lies down on the chill stone beside him, bringing her nearer to his dark face than she has ever been to any man's except when kissing him. And kissing, of course, is much in her mind, since if he breathes any more shallowly and imperceptibly than he is now doing she will have to seize him, tip back his head, and administer the kiss of life . . . his lips are full, and coloured like mulberries, but edged darker, as though drawn on his handsome face with a purple pencil. His eyelashes are coal black, flickering between open and shut against the whites of his eyes, and on his forehead the sheen of a fine sweat is showing. She touches him, gently brushing the hair back from his dank brow, and he opens his eyes, pits of darkness, the golden irises narrowed to fine bright rings round distended pupils.

'Help is coming,' she says softly. 'You'll be all right.'

'Hold me up a bit,' he says faintly, 'please.'

He is limp and heavy. She manages to raise him a little, and he puts his head into her lap, turns his face against her belly, and takes her free hand in both of his.

'How do you feel?' she asks him. His head is warm and heavy against her, and he is still breathing, though unevenly.

'Terrible,' he says, smiling weakly.

'Oh, I'm so sorry!' she cries, for it is entirely her fault – how could she have been so spectacularly stupid as to use a drinking glass to mix in – so crassly grossly stupid, and it was something she had been warned about too, in connection with the nasty things she had been taught to use. She might have killed him; – she still might, for he is still sweating, and is now beginning to retch slightly.

'I'm thirsty,' he whispers, pitifully. 'My mouth is burning.' But she does not know whether it would be safe to get him a drink.

She longs for Dora to come in; to need something from the house, and come in, and see, and help, and talk to her, but there is nothing but silence round her and the felled young man, until at long long last she hears the ringing footsteps of Roz returning in haste.

Dora goes singing down a garden alley, making towards the topiary garden, in which opposite a blurred Titania, a green, outgrowing Oberon, freed now of the rebellious bees, waits, unprotected against her pruning shears. She is carrying the shears and clippers over her arm in a basket, and although she has un-netted her hat, she is still wearing the bee-proof garb. Her path crosses another, deep between hedges, going to a peeling door at the foot of the west tower of the house – a Gothic affair, with ivy-blocked windows nearly to the top. But from the topmost window of this tower Alfie sees her come. He is staring bemused at William, who is lying face down in the grass in the crossing between the avenues of yew, instead of slipping back to Alfie, as he had been told to do, for further instructions. Ferdy had come half an hour ago, and with any luck is by now being stripped and laid naked in bed by Fleur, under strict instructions from the nurse; but William is simply lying out there flat on his face. Alfie has no wish at all to reveal himself, and be forced to explain his presence, so he stands at the window and watches. Dora is approaching, and in a few more steps will see

William stretched out . . . could the boy have guessed what to do next? Alfie cannot think what William is up to; he has never heard of anaphylactic shock. But luckily for William, Dora has.

So that when she sees the new gardener lying collapsed, she thinks at once, 'Oh, God, bee stings!' and runs to his side. He is having trouble breathing; a froth of sticky bubbles cobwebs his lips. His eyes are shut, and his forearms badly swollen. Dora was stung at the same time, but her stings are already subsiding into little rosy flecks . . . the gardener must be allergic. Dora looks round her frantically. She knows already that there is nobody in the garden, and how far it is back to any unlocked part of the house. She leans over the young man, and tears open the neck of his shirt, heaves him over on to his side, and then, looping up her skirt between her knees, revealing a slender pair of legs in white cotton trousers, she runs for the nearest wheelbarrow. As she runs, she tries to remember what she knows about first aid; she thinks she recalls that one ought not to let people slide into coma, and so when she gets the barrow back to the poor victim she slaps him roundly across both cheeks, and begins to enquire of him loudly where he lives, and how many brothers or sisters he has. She upends the barrow, and drags him on his back, trying to get him sitting against it. It isn't easy, and all the victim offers is a mutter or two, and rough breathing. At last she manages to make a kind of sling out of her skirt, tied round his chest under the arms, and with the aid of that to lean over between the handles of the upended barrow, and lift him into a sitting position against it. Then with a convulsive effort she rights the barrow, and the gardener, legs dangling over the front, head lolling on his half-propped trunk, is in it. She unties her skirt; he appears to be choking, and she doesn't like to leave it tightened round his chest. Then she begins to trundle the barrow, making away with it out of Alfie's fascinated view. She is struggling towards the back gate out onto the road, and once there flags down a motorist, and gets a lift to the nearest hospital. The car which stops for her contains a man and his wife, so she finds herself cradling her gardener in the back seat, staring anxiously at his flushed, fair skin, his eyelashes tinted with red, his fair curls. He fights to breathe in her arms, the indrawn breath short and shuddering, the breath out long and difficult.

'Oh, I'm so sorry,' she whispers to him. 'I didn't think . . .'

When the car pulls up at the casualty entrance she feels more relieved than ever before in her life. She knows that anaphylactic shock can cause death within the hour; but at least when she delivers him into the hands of experts the young man is still breathing.

'We simply don't know enough about it,' Thomas said.

'How could we find out?'

'We could try leading him on a bit in the next tutorial. We could warm him up by reading him some of the sort of stuff he likes to hear, we could flatter him a bit instead of disagreeing with him . . .'

'I'd choke!' said Anna.

'Well, but have you a better idea?'

'Not really.'

'I suppose we might have a chance of finding out which of Mr Lightdown's cronies might be open to it. I mean, I don't normally mix with the kind he likes; not much. But there aren't very many of them, and I know people who do know them. I could ask around and try to find a pair, and both with girl-friends.'

'But they might be people who have gone down,' she said.

'They might. But I should think going down waters down his influence a bit, and this pair, if they exist . . .'

'Are absolutely under his thumb. But, Thomas, it isn't any good just finding the men; they are in it up to their eyeballs; what could we say to them?'

'You want to find the girls, and warn them?'

'Yes!'

'Anna, do you think that would be easy? I mean, how would you react? Being warned against people usually works in their favour.'

'Even if you learn that they are lying and tricking you? Just a copy of the opera on their breakfast table would do it, I think!'

'So supposing this trick is really being played, what we need to know is where?'

'And then we go there. Or I do. I mean, will you help me, Thomas?'

'Always. In anything. In any way I can,' he said. 'You know that.'

'So the first step is pumping him. We have to be very bland with him, and agree with him, and put him off his guard.'

Thomas thought about it. 'If we suddenly start agreeing with him, he'll wonder why,' he said. 'I think we must just let him seem to convince us. He likes winning arguments. Can you manage that, Anna?'

'Of course I can,' she said, surprised.

'Well, it might not be entirely easy, and he does get across you rather.'

'But we'll only be pretending,' she said.

'Putting on a disguise?'

'As long as I know that you know I'm only pre-tending, I don't care what I say,' she said. 'I don't care a fig what he thinks!'

For a moment Thomas was cheered. Anna did care what he thought; he felt brave enough to kiss her softly on the cheek when she stood up to go. But in the cavernous emptiness of the room which she left behind her, the looming days to be traversed before the next tutorial, it seemed a very small consolation. However, she had definitely said it; for what it was worth, she cared more for Thomas's opinion than for Alfie's. Thomas took from the shelf his Oxford *Complete Shakespeare*, a slender volume in blue calf, on India paper, and turned to *Love's Labour's Lost*.

Telling Dora, at supper, about the catastrophe of the day, Fleur wonders whether to mention that the new assistant is an Indian. It seems to her that there is no discreet way of doing so. Why should Dora care, among so much dramatic detail, for that particular one? It's a sort of indelicacy to suppose so; it says, 'any of your kind must be interested in any other of your kind,' and is surely either racist – why should an English girl of Indian descent care to know about the descent of an assistant picture restorer? – or purely absurd, as when the shop assistant says to an Australian customer, 'My cousin is Australian; do you know her?' That the young man's race is in the forefront of her own mind is a side effect of seeing him naked, helping the nurse to get him into bed. For, undressed, he had not only appeared beauti-fully formed and proportioned, but his dark skin had the colour and patina of warm bronze, so that she might have been bedding the Donatello David, softened suddenly into comatose life. Not quite every part of the young man's person was limp and motionless in the process; and there was a startling livid empurplement of hue in his stirring part. Though she tried not to fix her gaze there, she noticed the strangeness of his dark, glossy, dead straight pubic hair. Then, no sooner had she and the mysterious nurse – for where had a nurse appeared from at such short notice? – got him decently covered, than he seized her hand, and kissed it, and murmured 'Treasure, beloved, treasure.'

'I hardly know him,' she had told the nurse. 'I only met him a couple of hours ago.'

'Don't let him bother you,' the nurse had said. 'It's the after-effect of the antidote I gave him. Patients often carry on like that. Best to humour him, really.'

Fleur had only extricated her hand from his by promising to visit him after supper. And now before she can apologize to Dora for opting out of the trip down to the pub for a drink they had expected to make, Dora is launched on explaining why she, Dora, must visit the local hospital instead. Dora is shaken, Fleur sees. Her bee sting crisis had lasted longer than the one over drinking solvent, and her gardener does seem to have been at death's door. The word 'gardener' evokes in Fleur's mind the image of an elderly man, with a face like a walnut, and moleskin trousers held up with string. The image she entertains as Dora tells her about the struggle to get the fellow into a wheelbarrow, and how heavy it was to wheel to the gate, has little correspondence with what Dora is remembering as she speaks; the image of the boy's golden head lolling backwards, his eyes opening and shutting, looking up at her as she struggles, as unexpectedly blue as those little butterflies that look like clippings of the sky. Pure embarrassment keeps Dora from mentioning that as he floated in and out of consciousness the young man had kept calling her an angel, and asking if he was in heaven.

'It was very awkward,' she tells Fleur instead, 'bringing someone into casualty, not knowing anything about them. His name? I haven't a clue. Religion? Don't know. Next of kin? Not me, I only just met him. Luckily it occurred to me to phone Roz, and Roz knew all about him. He is called Jim, and he has no family at all. The owner is his guardian in some way. Roz promised to let the owner know what has happened, but I am the only visitor he is likely to have this evening.'

'Oh, we've got to go and see them,' Fleur agrees. 'Visiting the sick. Fundamental duty, after all. But they aren't exactly brilliant assistants, are they? How much did you get done, what with all that?'

'Very little,' Dora says sadly. 'And when I get back I still have to deal with that swarm.'

'Do you think these jokers are all the helpers we are going to get,' Fleur wonders, 'or will there be others?'

'Oh, that's as clear as mud to me!' says Dora. 'I re-read the letter I got from the owner. I can't tell. It seems to me now to be very vague. Frankly, anything seems possible in this place!'

'And yet,' Fleur muses, helping herself to a plateful of the chicken swimming in tarragon and cream set out for their supper, 'if this house were set to rights, it would be one of the most beautiful country houses in England, and very interesting. A demonstration of the development of style.'

'The garden is wonderful too,' says Dora. 'The parts near the house were laid out before 1700, I think, and are full of old rare plants. It's a scholarly garden, it must have had botanists tending it; really it should never have been allowed to run wild . . . and then, beyond all the formal bit, there's a spectacular collection of rhododendrons round the lake – that must have taken most of Victoria's reign to establish.'

'So which bit of the house do you prefer?' Fleur asks.

'Well, the front is very beautiful; admirable, I would say. And the Gothic bit is really rather absurd, but if I had to live here, I would choose rooms at the back. I expect it's very vulgar of me, isn't it?'

'Perhaps. But I would, too. The Palladian order seems both cool and somehow demanding.'

'And the garden, Fleur? Which bit of the garden would you rather walk in?'

'Oh, through the woodland plantation by the lake. I can see that all the courtyards of yew are interesting, but they seem somehow rather sinister. Don't you think so? Nature cut and pruned into what it's not. I prefer things natural.'

'Well neither kind of garden is natural. Nettles and bindweed are that. Is that the time?'

They are eating supper still in their working clothes, both having been made late by the afternoon's dramas. Now Fleur pushes back her chair, and says, 'I'm going to change before I go visiting. And you? Can we find two bathrooms?'

'There must be dozens, all antique!' says Dora.

Lying tucked into an immaculate bed, in a high bedroom, Ferdy has time to think. He is recovering from nausea; though he did not actually drink the stuff in the glass, the smell of the fluids he spilt, the fumes from the spillage that he had been forced to breathe as he lay feigning on the floor, have gone to his stomach. It is lucky for him, he reflects, that William's girl reeks of chemicals, and looks like a factory worker; being manhandled by her might otherwise have been too much for his self-possession. By contrast he thinks tenderly of Dora, so delicate, so gentle . . . just the thought that she is somewhere near, under the same roof, fills him with joy. Even if he cannot see her, cannot speak to her, the knowledge of her nearness refreshes him, like the airs of a summer day in a scented garden . . . he closes his eyes, and imagines her, walking in an alley of roses, cutting off the overblown heads, and gathering them in a basket. He is walking by her side. As she goes the buds break open, unfurling, eager to be ripe enough for her shears . . .

'How are you feeling?' says a voice.

At the foot of the bed stands a young woman whom he does not at first recognize. He blinks at her. Her hair is thick and golden, curling to her shoulders, she is wearing a flowered dress, and pearls, and is gazing at him with the expression of unguarded candour one sees on Renaissance virgins in fresco. She smells not of acetate, but of some fruity soap, a smell of apples, or apricots; if she were a painting he would admire her beauty to the limit; in the flesh she is not his type at all, and the thought of those clear grey eyes having scanned him top to toe this afternoon has him cringing, but at least William's infatuation is comprehensible now. He remembers what he ought to do, and reaches out a hand to her, saying, 'Dearest!'

'Oh, come now, I thought you had recovered,' she says, but her steady stare does not waver. 'I don't even know your name, do you realize?'

'Shiva,' he lies. 'Shiv, for short.'

'I've met someone else called Shiva,' she says.

'It's quite a usual name. It is the name of the God

of cosmic energy – what you would call the Life Force, I think. Won't you sit down?'

There is nothing to sit on except the bed. She perches on the edge. 'Well, Shiv, how are you feeling?'

'Oh, I'm better. I'll be up tomorrow, and well enough to take you out to dinner.'

'We'll see about that when we see how the work goes,' she says coolly.

'I don't think I would be well enough to work,' he says, 'if it were not the only way to make you let me spend the day with you.'

'I simply don't know how to deal with you,' she says. 'You are outside my social scope altogether. It isn't gentlemanly to keep on like that when I've asked you to stop.'

'I can't help it,' he offers. 'You drive me crazy with desire. Why do you think I drank that lethal stuff? Your nearness had overpowered my presence of mind.'

'Well, nothing seems to stop your flow of talk,' she says, getting up. 'I think you'll live. Is there anything I can do for you?'

'Kiss me.'

'I meant, is there anyone I should telephone, anything you urgently need?'

'A kiss. I am dying of longing for one. Please. Just one; just goodnight . . . have pity on me . . .'

He stretches out his arms to her, with an expression of theatrical longing on his face. Such a witty, expressive face, and there is always the glint of laughter in his eyes. It gives him away, really. She knows he is only fooling. And it isn't very likeable, she thinks, to meet affectionate fooling with serious denial. She goes to him, meaning to lean over him like his mother, and bestow a kiss on his forehead, but he takes her head between his hands, holds her firmly, and diverts it, pressing her lips against his. Only when his tongue comes into play does she break free, saying, 'You do push your luck!' and stalking out.

Jim-William, meanwhile is being visited in D Ward by a woman he has never clapped eyes on before. The bee-veil had masked her completely from view; now he sees a vision with an oval face, perfectly proportioned, huge dark eyes, a calm brow, thick blue-black hair in a long plait, and a slightness of build that makes him amazed to think she was able to hoist him and trundle him towards help and rescue.

'You saved my life,' he says.

'No, no,' she answers. 'Nearly lost it, rather. Why didn't you tell me you were allergic to stings?' Her voice is soft and low pitched, and with a slight huskiness. An oboe.

'I didn't know,' he says.

'Good god! Then we are both very lucky.'

'Would you have grieved, then, if I had died?'

'What do you take me for? Of course I would! It would have been horrible.'

'Then you are not wholly indifferent to me?'

'I'm not that indifferent to anybody!' she retorts.

'Dearest Dora,' he says, 'the moment they let me out of here, I'm going to take you out and feast you, and buy you presents, and champagne, and dance with you, and . . .'

'Hold on, hold on. I take it bee stings haven't made you forget that I am betrothed?'

'But it would only be to thank you for saving my life! Is this fiancé of yours a monster? What harm would it do? Darling, please. You don't know how I long for a kind word from you, how I long to make you smile.' And it's true, he thinks, surprised at himself, I would love to see her smile!

'I'll think about it,' she says. 'But I'll go now, before you get over-excited.'

'Kiss me goodnight?'

'Certainly not.'

'I shall be the only man in the ward who doesn't get a goodnight kiss,' he said, pouting like a little boy.

'Then you must be the only one whose visitor is someone else's girl,' she says crisply, going.

William turns his head on the pillow to watch her out of sight. She is wearing, he sees, a midnight blue sari, in which she seems to float sinuously rather than simply walking.

'She's absolutely stunning!' he tells himself. 'Lucky Ferdy! And very cool; I wonder how Ferdy thawed the ice-maiden act?'

'What do you want?' enquires a voice from the foot of the bed. Jim-William blinks.

'Tea, coffee, chocolate, Horlicks?'

'Tea,' says William, dreamily, 'as long as it's Indian.'

'It's a Tetley tea-bag,' says the nurse. 'All right?'

Fleur stands thunderstruck, half way down the stairs. It has occurred to her that she has not spent a single minute of the whole day thinking about William. She hasn't yearned for him, she hasn't missed him, he simply hasn't crossed her mind at all; and yet last night she cried herself to sleep for him! She is horrified at herself. But it is certainly true that her thoughts have been otherwise employed; first on the painting, then the accident, then . . . Shiv's kiss is still palpable on her lips. She presses her mouth hard on to the back of her hand, though whether to imprint or erase the tactile memory she hardly knows. And, worse and worse, when she snatches at the memory of William to steady her she cannot retrieve an image of his face; a smile, a profile, his left eye in close-up – fragments of him flicker and blur in her mind, and will not cohere, will not come whole. She races on, down to the landing, along the endless galleries, up the tower stairs to her bedroom, going for his photograph as though for a life raft to save herself.

And it does calm her. William's handsome face in close-up, deeply smiling, looks back at her. Dear, dear William; so brave and loving! How could she have kissed a stranger within a few hours of his departure? But, to her confusion, she finds that the aching inner yearning which possesses her switches freely to the image of Shiv, reaching up to kiss her, holding her head between his strong hands, and the image of William. But what would she herself feel if she found that William had been kissing another girl? Fleur sits down, and thinks hard. She knows very well that she does not expect William to be kissing anyone else, or even trying to kiss anyone else. That does not fall within her view of what is expected of a fiancé. Or, never mind the engagement, what she expects of someone who has declared himself in love with her. Obviously, then, in symmetry she would expect William to be deeply hurt at her letting Shiv kiss her, and she would not really expect him to accept as an excuse the eagerness with which Shiv had been pursuing her, or the appeal to her softheartedness arising from his skirmish with death at her hands. Or would she?

Wait a bit. She would, now she comes to think of it, expect a man to be partly at least pleased to have his girl pursued avidly by others; to have others envy him and compete with him – who would not rather own something greatly desired by other people? William, who is tolerant, and as well-tempered as that famous clavier, probably wouldn't even mind much if she humoured the indefatigable Shiv; nor could she imagine him expecting anything but kindness in her towards any other person . . . though she flinches, Fleur forces herself to confront the heart of the matter. Of course William wouldn't mind her kissing Shiv – as long as she didn't want to. Giving in briefly to persuasion was one thing; giving in to herself was quite another!

Getting up, she paces between the beds, and glances at the prospect of the garden, darkening through the window. 'If only Dora would come home! I need someone to talk to, to stop me thinking,' she tells herself. 'Why should I be afraid of thinking?' She sits down again.

The truth is that Shiv arouses desire. It must be lust, of course; love, she had been led to suppose, takes longer, and requires that one should know the person, at least somewhat. And lust for a new acquaintance should have been prevented by love; she had always supposed that being in love simply eliminated this sort of thing, that when you were in love fidelity came as naturally as breathing. Very well, then, it was not so. Random encounters would still arouse longing, dreaming, alarmingly specific hungers . . . one would have to control them after being in love, as, presumably, one had done before. Oddly, Fleur, who has liked many young men, cannot remember having this sort of problem before. Of course, she has never before stripped a young man and put him naked between the sheets . . . no!, she wrenches her thoughts angrily away from that enticing recollection, and, she warns herself, before her thoughts get that far, that he is not really lying alone upstairs longing for her; that nurse is around somewhere.

The nurse is puzzling. When Fleur asked her why

Shiv was in such a remote room the nurse had replied that it was convenient, because her other patient was nearby. Another patient?

'I haven't heard any mad laughter!' Fleur had said.

'Pardon?' said the nurse.

They had been standing at the door of Shiv's room, talking in low voices, though Shiv was wide awake, and indeed was staring yearningly at Fleur all the while. 'Oh, for God's sake, Fleur!' she tells herself, furious at her failure to control her thoughts. 'The fact is, something I thought would be easy is going to be difficult. That's all. I shall need to watch myself. Being in love doesn't warn off other people, it almost seems to give *him* a green light, and it doesn't warn off me! But it is William I love. I promised to love him, and I do love him, and I shall be true to that.' As to dealing with that delicious, and irrepressible, and unavoidable assistant, the heart of the matter, she realizes, is not what William, if he knew, would expect of her, but what she expects of herself.

At this, Dora still not having returned, having had enough of solitary thinking, Fleur pulls a shawl round her shoulders, and sets off through the house and into the dusky garden to meet her.

The garden is not as dark as from the house it had seemed. Though outlines of plants and bushes are vague, as in a sort of Stygian mist, flowers show faintly definite, and the perfumes they reserve for the quiet hours, for the night-fliers who court them under cover of darkness, are vividly sweet. Dora's car is in the drive, but there is no sign of her, and Fleur strides down a shadowy path, calling. At the far end of the garden, through an archway clipped in a dark hedge, and across an orchard in which a bird sings ravishingly in a brilliant cadenza, Dora finally answers, 'Over here!'

'Whatever are you doing so late?' Fleur asks,

going to her through the thick uncut grass, so that her shoes are soaked through. 'Surely you're not working at this hour?'

'I have to see the bees safe,' says Dora. 'All the stragglers come in at night. The morning is too late.'

'Don't you need a veil? Won't they sting us?'

'No. They are happy when they swarm. You can watch this.'

Dora props a sheet of plywood at a gentle slope going up to the door of the hive. Then she skips off for a moment, and comes back carrying an inverted cardboard box. Gently she puts it at the foot of the wooden ramp, and props it, leaving a space below the bottom of the box. And then she slaps the top of the box, hard. The box rustles, and the bees pour out of it. Fleur, her eyes wide in the dimness, sees with asonishment an army of bees advancing on the hive. They have a leader; they form a perfect triangle with the apex marching towards the hive door. The march goes on and on, and finishes with a few stragglers. Dora picks up the box, knocks the bottom out of it, and flattens it. 'All right,' she says.

'How do you know they'll go in?' asks Fleur.

'It's baited with candy cake, and a little honey. It's warm and dry, and full of foundations for their combs; they know a good thing when they see it.'

'Somehow it scares me a bit to see how orderly they are!'

'They are truly mysterious,' Dora agrees. 'One can ask them things; did you know that?'

'Ask them? What sort of things?'

'One talks to them. Perhaps they are pleased. They make more honey. Perhaps they are not. They hum, and fly around at random. But they always like to know.'

'Well, go on, then; ask them something!'

'Bees! Bees!' calls Dora. 'Would it be all right to go

out to dinner with Jim? To go out like a western girl, and have fun? Would it?'

The bees are silent. Fleur puts an arm round Dora's waist, and they walk together under the apple boughs, and into the shade of the alleys of yew. Above their heads the stars are bright. The looming bulk of the house – no lights in the windows – offers a questionable welcome. They walk close together, Dora leaning against Fleur.

'What is he like?'

'He is very nice,' says Dora softly.

'Your gardener?'

'A nice young man. He says he only wants to thank me. Would it be all right?'

'Were you asking me?' says Fleur. 'I thought you were asking the bees!'

'But tell me. I am in between two ways of thinking. I am not sure what I would do if I were an English girl with English family. But I think I would feel free to go to dinner.'

Fleur does not answer her. Dismay engulfs her. In the darkness the front of the house is invisible, but the Gothic towers stand out against the sky. There must be more of them than she had realized; it looks like an enchanted castle in a fairy story. She had assumed that Dora would take a severe view of their shared pre-empted state, would be, therefore, an ally against temptation; if Dora wavers, how hard it will be not to succumb!

'Tell me, dear friend,' says Dora, as they ascend the suddenly moonlit steps to the great door, as the moon shows them the balanced and elegant façade muted and insubstantial in the dim radiance. 'If you were me, what would you do?'

'I wouldn't go!' cries Fleur, 'I would, I mean I wouldn't dream of it!' And she steps free of Dora's soft clasp.

She has put silence between them. And later, when Dora is safely sleeping, she herself cannot sleep. Nor can she, without a light to see William's picture by, address her troubled thoughts to the image of the right man. At last she gets up, puts on her dressing gown, and descends into the ghostly house. Wherever the moonlight gets in the rooms are decipherable in a pallid glory; elsewhere the darkness challenges her to know her way. Amorphous shapes loom palely in her path. She enters the music room, and puts the lights on. A crystal candelabrum casts a brightly speckled light on the panel she had been working on. She should wait, really, for better illumination. But she stares at the figure of the man in dark velvet that had so excited her and Shiv earlier. He is cleaned and clear now, almost to shoulder height, standing against a fold of curtain, looking on. She places the ladder close, and mixes a little more of the solvent gel. Then she begins to clean the hidden face.

She is working with certain assumptions, though also with irrational anxiety. The posture and position of the figure in the picture suggests that it is that of an older man; a friend, perhaps a father even, of the two young women. They must know he is there, behind them. But he does not exactly share the action depicted; whoever they are waving at, he stands too far back to see; it is them he watches . . . and nothing prepares Fleur for what her sponge uncovers. The onlooker's expression is one of unholy demonic laughter, of savage glee.

Anna lay on her bed, staring at the ceiling. A pattern of shadows from the plane trees in front of her window danced across her, casting the shapes of leaves and the little bobbing baubles of the seed clusters, one of which trembled over her right nipple, as though her shirt were translucent. She held in her hand a creamy deckle-edged card from Alfie, college-crested in full colour, on which was written in his crabbed black hand, 'For next week, an essay of the usual length, please, on fidelity. Lightdown.'

So Anna was supposed to be thinking about fidelity, and was actually thinking about Thomas. She couldn't help it really; she had only ever received one offer of undying love, and that had come from Thomas. Anna recalled it, working slowly and carefully through the afternoon when it had happened. She had been, of course, in an experimental mood. She had dressed up precisely in order to see what would happen; and, oddly, it seemed to her now, she had not been entirely clear that whatever happened would be happening to her. She winced now, clear-minded, at the delusion. Had she thought that she could put on virginity again as she took off her fancy dress? The truth was that she had been carried away with the idea of proving that disguises could not work; she had been playing a game. And it had been good fun! She had bought the motorcyclist's jacket from the charity shop; the tight leather trousers had been borrowed from the girl at the end of the corridor; the haircut, the hair colouring and the safety pin were all fixed up at a hairdresser's by the station, called 'Freak-Out', where they had been amazed that she hadn't known that the safety pins didn't really pierce through flesh. Or that they didn't have to; they had told her some bloodcurdling tales. Then she had emerged transformed, and walked through Oxford. She had lolled against a lamp-post outside the lecture rooms, as the morning lectures ended, and been passed ungreeted and unrecognized by a dozen or more acquaintances. Then she had trotted off to try Thomas. Still in an experimental mood. Exhilarated, flying free.

And, of course, if you are trying to see what happens, you don't stop it happening the moment it starts. Anna had let Thomas do to the punk girl what she would certainly not have let him do to herself . . . No, that was not true either. She had let him do to the punk girl what, now it had been done to the punk girl, she knew she wanted him to do again and again, for ever and ever, to her. Though it was unclear to her how, as herself, she could have found that out. As herself she hadn't been very good at being seduced. She had, she now thought, been issued with a misleading instruction book, as had the one or two young men who had attempted her before. Since she seemed to be not, as she had been told most women are, sluggish and slow to get going, but unmanageably fast. She could now see, looking back on those prehistoric encounters, that her wooers had taken so long petting, sighing, working themselves up to it, that her own excitement had died down in sheer boredom. Foreplay made her feel as unappetizing as a fish on a slab. Whereas Thomas had been so wonderfully quick!

Smiling deeply, she remembered the joy of being found irresistible. With amazement she remembered that she had easily caught up with him. It was not supposed to be easy, except when one was drunk. And what had intoxicated her, of course, was the heady power of her disguise.

Anna's smile vanished. She was bravely bringing her thoughts to bear on what happened afterwards. For the truth was that Thomas seemed to find her more resistible at every encounter. She could feel the tug of some force between them, but she could also feel him holding back. Not just trying to hold back, but succeeding. As Anna, she was not desired, and as for the punk girl – *Poor Thomas, he had better love a dream.* Where, then, did that leave fidelity? Thomas, in the heat of the moment, or perhaps in the melting ecstasy of the moment after, had rashly promised it, and it appeared just the same that he was not held by it, not for three days, never mind for a lifetime. But then, he had promised it to the punk girl, not to her.

Struggling to surface through the tide of misery this thought induced – she had not till now known, she thought, what it was to feel unhappiness – she got up, took her coat from the hook behind the door, and went in search of friends to talk to.

She found Margery reading in front of the communal washing machine in the basement. The soapflecks spattered the screen like after-hours television, when the set is left with nothing but the universe to tune into. 'I've been looking for you,' she said.

'Okay,' said Margery. 'The book isn't much more riveting than the show.'

'What is it?'

Margery showed her the title page. *'Teleology in Genetics: A Critique.'*

'Cor. What's teleology?'

'The idea that things have a purpose.'

'Well, don't they?'

'Probably not. I mean, what is a frog for, would you say? Or what are you for?'

'Oh, I see what you mean. You mean what's the use of us, froggy and me? I thought you meant purpose, as in intention. After all, a frog can want to cross the road, or get himself kissed by a princess, and I . . .'

'You can form an intention. Right, but that wouldn't make you, complete with intentions, *for* anything.'

104

'I thought you were a biologist, not a philosopher.'

'This is biology. If I ask you what are a bird's wings for . . .'

'Flying.'

'. . . you will say "flying". As if someone or somebody intended birds to fly, and therefore gave them wings. Did you want me for anything?'

'I wanted help. I'm stuck with an essay. It's on fidelity.'

'I thought you were a musicologist, not a theologian.'

'This is musicology. Be a pal. Tell me what fidelity is for.'

'Easy-peasy. It's for bamboozling males into helping with the rearing of young. Next question?'

'Wait. Explain.'

'Well, let's assume that the overriding purpose of individuals is to reproduce themselves. Don't argue; just assume that.'

'If you say so.'

'Then the interests of male individuals would be best served by impregnating the maximum number of females, thus giving their genes the maximum number of chances in the survival stakes . . . but females don't need to be impregnated by lots of males. Once is enough. What they need is some help and protection while they are defenceless, nesting or heavily pregnant and, if possible, help in feeding and rearing the young. So they will try to find a mate who will provide that help; this will give males willing to provide help an advantage in the marriage market, which may make the giving of help worthwhile. Of course, if the male helps to raise the young, then his genes in those young will get a better chance; but if he gets himself other young on the side, those may survive too, giving his genes bonus chances.'

'So you're saying that the idea of fidelity is a conspiracy, put about by women to induce men to behave to the advantage of their children?'

'Yes. But of course, the most successful imaginable male, from the point of view of his genes, would be, say, bigamously raising and protecting two families, or one very large one, or even two very large ones if he can manage it, and getting the maximum number of bastards on the side. That's why there's a double standard; it simply doesn't matter much if a man is sexually unfaithful, as long as he continues to support his legitimate offspring. His wife is likely to forgive him as long as the housekeeping money is intact. Help me heave this lot into the dryer.'

'And these repulsive ideas are underwritten by biology?' Anna asked, once they were looking at the slow kaleidoscope of clothes lumbering round.

'Seem to be. Don't let it put you off.'

'Thanks,' said Anna. 'You've been a great help.'

Climbing the stairs, away from the rumbling dryer, and the crude perfume of soap powder, she thought about it. And swiftly latched on to what was preposterous, what had stung her, in what Margery said. For females, 'once is enough.' Oh, no. No ... reeling with thoughts of Thomas, she climbed the stairs to the upper floor where Laura's room was.

Laura was spread out on her window seat, in a room awash with Tchaikovsky.

'Fidelity,' said Anna, sitting in the armchair.

'Have nothing to do with it,' said Laura.

'Most likely,' said Anna, 'when I've finished this essay, I won't. But why?'

'Male capitalist plot,' said Laura, reaching out to turn down the anguished sound.

'I thought it was a cardinal virtue,' said Anna, lowering her voice as she found herself shouting, now that Tchaikovsky was moaning instead of howling.

'Ask yourself why it is expected only of women.'

'But surely fidelity is admired also in men?'

'Fidelity to a cause, or to a superior officer, yes. Fidelity to a woman is just rather wimpish.'

'But . . .'

'Naturally; fidelity in men serves no purpose.'

'Is this one of your Marxist theories?'

'It's plain common sense. There is, of course, an official myth, which everyone subscribes to. The myth enjoins mutual fidelity in marriage. Men insist very heavily on that in their wives, because they've got to have chaste wives if they want to be sure that the children they are raising are their own. The whole appalling seclusion of women, their confinement to the home, the limits on their lives, the protective treatment of them as if they were babies or idiots, the ruthless punishment and ostracism of those who stray from respectability – the whole traditional system is intended to make sure that the father's property descends to his own son. The whole stupid, cruel ideology is about property, not about morality or happiness.'

'But, Laura, surely faithfulness does make people happy?'

'Ho, ho,' said Laura darkly. 'They've got you duped, I see.'

'Who have?'

'Well, the system has. And those who benefit from it.'

'Hasn't it changed a bit in our times, don't you think?'

'Because you see fathers pushing babies round supermarkets? Look closer.'

But Anna didn't want to get into an interminable argument with Laura about the position of women.

'What did you mean by saying men insist on it? Don't women demand it too?'

'They delude themselves. The official myth expects men to be faithful too, because it would collapse if it were too visibly unfair. But there isn't any power behind the prohibition for them. No social ostracism, no penalty. It's even rather amusing: a philanderer is a devil of a fellow, and a wife who refuses to forgive is not thought of as in the right, just as a spiteful bitch.'

'Oh, Laura, surely . . .'

'Because, you see, it doesn't in the least matter if men are unfaithful. It takes a long time for these atavistic value sets to change, and until very recently a bastard couldn't inherit. Female infidelity did, and male infidelity did not, threaten the descent of property. Only fear of the pox restrained them, and if fear of AIDS hadn't replaced it, they would behave even worse.'

'So you are saying that the ideal of fidelity is a conspiracy perpetrated by men against women to secure the descent of property down a legitimate line?'

'Right. Hooray. I thought you weren't quite getting it.'

'And is this how you feel about Jake?' Anna asked, naming Laura's boyfriend.

'Absolutely typical of a soggy liberal!' said Laura. 'It's different for me and Jake.'

'Why?'

'We are talking about a vast con-trick. Once you see through the fraud being perpetrated by capitalism, however, you are free.'

'So you wouldn't mind a bit if Jake dumped you and ran off with someone else?'

'You're so personal all the time, Anna. It's the liberal fallacy to think that personal feelings matter. They don't. What's all this about, anyway?'

'An essay. I was stuck.'

'On *Figaro*, no doubt. Listen, Anna. *Figaro* is a wonderful example of the vicious nature of bourgeois art.'

'It was thought rather revolutionary in its time,' Anna said.

'Well, but think about it. There's the scene at the end in which the dirty old Count is down on his knees asking forgiveness. Everybody knows he doesn't mean it. He'll be groping the chambermaids again by the morning. And the Countess ought to pay him out; but she forgives him. I ask you! Just the sort of thing we're talking about. And then that shit Mozart surrounds the whole thing with wonderful music, supporting it, making it convincing, getting it under your skin – all that beauty was in the service of the corrupt – don't you see? Art propping up the tyranny of the system. That's what you ought to put in your essay.'

'Yes, Laura,' Anna said, getting up. 'Thank you very much, that's a great help. Incidentally, is Tchaikovsky quite your cup of tea?'

'What do you mean?' said Laura.

'Well, if personal feelings aren't important, should you be stroking them and stirring them up with this stuff?'

'Oh,' said Laura. 'I see. Well, I suppose feelings help one to keep going, on a day-to-day basis. That must be what they are for. But individuals don't matter; only society matters.'

Anna fled, saying, 'There's a spot of teleology there, Laura!' And she felt none the wiser. What were feelings for? Did someone or something give them to us, as it gave birds wings? What was love for, anyway? She could always, of course, go and talk to Thomas. But instead she put on her jacket, put a toothbrush in the pocket, and went down to

Gloucester Green bus station, where she boarded a bus home. She was going to talk to her mother.

Hot croissants wrapped in white napkins, fragrant black coffee, hard boiled quails' eggs, and kedgeree in blue and white Chinese porcelain bowls are laid out ready for them in the morning. Roz pours orange juice for them, and sits down with them comfortably in the third chair at the table.

'I take it I am not to make supper for tonight?' she says.

'Oh?' says Fleur.

'A little bird tells me you are both invited out this evening,' says Roz, smiling.

'But we have not decided whether to go,' says Fleur.

'What a strange pair you are!' says Roz.

'But what are you after?' cries Fleur. 'Why does it matter to you?'

'Well it doesn't. Of course you can tell me to mind my own business. It's just that I am taking a friendly interest in you both. I am supposed to look after you, keep you comfortable, keep you happy. A little company seems likely to cheer you up – if you're normal young women, that is.'

'Well, be patient with me, Roz, since I have a foreign background, you know,' says Dora, 'and explain to me what a normal young woman would do. Being, of course, engaged.'

'Ah, take things a little lightly!' says Roz, smiling at Dora. 'You are so serious! There is a time for earnestness, no doubt; but you need to know when to relent a bit. You trust your Fernando completely, of course, but a little foresight, and you'd be ready to hedge your bet.'

'But what do you mean by hedging the bet?' demands Fleur.

'Take the chances that offer. Flirt a little; have fun!'

'That may be what Roz would do, Dora,' says Fleur, dismayed, 'but . . .'

'It's what I do do. Use a little womanly cunning.'

'Like what, Roz?' says Dora. Her eyes are bright, and an expression of eagerness lights them.

'Heavens, any grown woman should know!' Roz says. 'You are both beautiful – let it shine, let it give pleasure. With glances, and laughter, and play-acting desire or distress you can please everyone, please dozens at a time. You can have every man within miles of you dancing attendance – young or old, handsome or ugly, you can make yourself reckoned with. Go on; go out to dinner!'

'And then?' asks Dora.

'What do you think?'

'Won't it go further? Won't they press us further? What will we do then?'

'Why, whatever you like!' says Roz, laughing. She gets up, and fetches from the sideboard an oval bowl of creamy china, a lovely thing with a cut-out pattern of trellis-work, twined through with vines and leaves. It is full of pale green apples, and fresh figs, with a soft bloom on the swelling purple skins. She sets the bowl down on the table, and chooses a fig. 'You could eat the figs now,' she says, pulling it open, and recurving the petals of its ruptured skin like a Turk's-cap lily. They watch her suck at the exposed pink flesh. 'And keep the apples for later!'

'Well, what do you make of that?' Fleur asks Dora as they climb the stairs, going to change into working clothes for the day.

'It certainly sounds a bit mad to my ears,' says Dora. 'Do you think we could do as she says?'

'But wouldn't it be wrong for us, being engaged?'

'That's the whole question – what would we be doing wrong?'

'Well, ask yourself what your fiancé would say if he found out.'

'But my dear Fleur, how could he, how could they, possibly find out? On St Kilda? And if they did hear that we had had dinner with our assistants, what then?'

'And in your secret heart of hearts?'

'I feel exactly as before. Cheering ourselves up instead of mooching around here being gloomy in our time off isn't breaking our word, is it?'

'Well, no,' says Fleur, struggling with inner panic. She knows full well her own secret heart is far from trustworthy.

'So, are we accepting invitations for tonight? I will if you will.'

'All right,' says Fleur. 'But don't blame me if it all goes wrong!'

Someone has been moving things in the music room. A dustsheet has been hung across the end of the room, perhaps to protect the piano. Rather conveniently, the ladders have been moved, and the platform of two planks is standing against the second panel, just where she wants it. Thoughtfully Fleur mixes her solvents, taking care this time to use only beakers for the stuff, though Shiv is presumably still in bed, and surely wouldn't do such a thing twice. She is reminded obscurely of the statue of Laocoon, called into her mind by the struggle not to think of Shiv.

The second panel shows two young women – the same two, she supposes – in a small garden, with plants in elaborate pots. With them are two men in brilliant and elaborate exotic costume – flowing cloaks, slashed and embroidered sleeves, enormous headgear of some kind. The men are holding out their hands to the girls, and pointing to a blur of colour seen through a delicate columned arcade. Fleur studies the shadows, and finds, in an archway, the expected dark onlooker. He can wait. She shudders, remembering the shock his expression gave her when she uncovered it late last night. She begins work instead on the flowery blur through the arches. A garlanded boat emerges, laden with flowers, and swan-necked like a gondola. A white dove is perched on the gilded top strake, piles of silken cushions can be seen, and a shadowy gondolier is standing in the stern. The gesture of the men, bowing, pointing, is an unmistakable invitation to embark.

And as she begins to clean, to bring up the dazzling autumnal colours of the dark boat and its bright cargo, music, very soft at first, but still startling, fills the room. She strides over to the dustsheet, and tweaks it, whereupon it falls, revealing a pianist playing behind it.

'Whatever . . . ?' she says, and the pianist, without ceasing to play, briefly gestures at a note propped on the piano lid. 'If music be the food of love – relent and dine with me tonight. S.'

'Oh, really!' she exclaims. 'What am I to do about this?' She sees that the note has a tiny 'PTO' at the bottom. On the other side is written, 'It gives delight, and hurts not!'

'But I have to work,' she says aloud, and returns to the ladder. Exquisite sound fills the room. The picture seems less heavily dirtied than the first panel, and she is working fast. Under her sponges the figure of the man in the centre of the panel emerges in preposterous brilliance. But when she

113

reaches the face, she withholds the biting solvent, and hesitates. The figure is wearing a mask. But it is not of the same paint at all as the rest of the picture. Most of the surface of the panels has been done in a very competent fresco, and is fused with the surface of the plaster. The mask has been painted on later, in secco.

Fleur descends from the ladder, and drags it across the floor, removing it from in front of the panel. She stands back and contemplates the picture intently. Music flows round her, but she is oblivious of it. One might take the view that the job of the restorer is simply to restore the picture to its original state. The original artist of these murals must have painted a face on the exotic figure; and the face might have been as powerfully expressive as the face full of devilment on the onlooker in the first picture; the artist was capable of it. Why had a mask been added? Warning bells sound loudly in her mind. Her training in restoration had been full of tales of people who cleaned off work by such as Van Eyck, to reveal below the third-rate work of artists whose old canvases the mighty had re-used. There is no reason to think that the bottom layer is the best.

She decides to clean the other faces in the picture first. She is deeply absorbed, excited by the task. The music plucks at her attention with its shimmering flow, and she shuts it out of her mind.

An hour later she can look again. Both men are masked; both girls are barefaced. One of the girls is looking away from the man who beckons her, but smiling, half concealing the smile with the coquettish turn of the head. But once again the painter surprises her. For the expression on the face of the second girl is one of anguish. She stares at her masked companion, head held high, and tears in her eyes. At odds with the whole feeling of the

114

picture. Much more tempted than before to clean off the mask, which perhaps covers up the reason for this strangeness, yet thinking that she should really consult the owner over a matter such as this, Fleur hesitates. Could she, if removing the mask proves to be not welcome, simply paint a new one back on?

The music has ceased. 'I would have him serenade you all day, if he were not needed somewhere else for a rehearsal.' The voice breaks her reverie, and she sees that the piano player has finished, and is packing up his sheet music, and that Shiv has appeared beside her. 'Advise me,' she asks him. 'How far should this go?'

'It's a serious matter, unmasking someone,' he says. 'A big step. Playing along with them might be more fun. And that stuff does smell nauseating; couldn't we go for a walk together?'

Thomas was full of unease. He hadn't seen Anna for days, and somehow he had expected to see her, expected that she would consult him about her essay, about the scheme to play along with Mr Lightdown. Thomas had been from the first unsure that Anna would be able to pretend compliance with an average dose of iconoclasm from Lightdown. But she hadn't dropped in to talk, though the coffee had been waiting all week, and he had opened the door with a beating heart to every knock. Now he was hanging about, waiting for her in the garden that she would cross to Lightdown's room. His own essay was tucked into a folder under his arm. When she came, he reached out and took her hand.

'How has it been?' he asked. 'Plan One still on?'

'I suppose so,' she said. She did not withdraw her hand, which lay soft and rather cool in his, but she did not look at him. He felt irrationally anxious about her, but they were already climbing the stairs, and there was no time to talk. Moments later they were disposed at each end of Lightdown's sofa, ready to read.

'It would be only fair, this time, to take ladies first,' said Lightdown, with a surprising recall. 'Anna?'

So Anna read. 'In the first place it is difficult to be absolutely clear exactly what degree of obligation the four characters in *Cosi* are under. They are not married; only engaged to be married, though they use the words "*sposi*" of each other repeatedly. Only once in the text of the opera is "*promessi sposi*" used as a description of the absent men. To break an engagement is presumably everywhere and at all times a much less awful crime than to break marriage vows; the slippery use of the words in the libretto is in fact a literary device with which Da Ponte deliberately confuses the question of exactly how heinous a crime it is if the sisters go off with new partners. The breaking of marriage vows, which seems only too likely to follow the imprudence of the conduct of the pairs during the time-span of the opera, is not an issue here, and neither is the massive question of the obligations towards children which lie on parents. The characters have not uttered to each other the stupendous promises of the marriage service, they have merely promised that they will promise. It is interesting to note that although the opera does bring everyone to the brink of marriage, here too, when one looks closely there are ambiguities. What takes place on stage is a civil ceremony – a signing of a marriage contract, not a church ceremony with the numinous resonance of vows before God. That would be altogether too serious in tone for the opera, which deals with serious matters by means of little prickles of unease evoked in the audience by the course of a story which seems light and frivolous all through. But the contract which is signed on stage is the phoney one that binds the girls to marry the Albanians. Had they already signed such a contract with the two men before their departure to the wars? Or are they about to sign one when the curtain falls? How seriously are we to regard the keeping or breaking of such signed contracts? Mozart himself signed a contract of marriage. He took communion with his future wife on the second of August, 1782, signed a marriage contract on the third, and got married on the fourth, at St Stephen's Cathedral. Clearly the contract, however important it was, was not the marriage. And Da Ponte, who is probably the one responsible for the ambiguities under discussion, never got married at all, of course, being debarred by his ordination.'

'My dear girl,' said Alfie, breaking in, 'you are as always, wonderful for your application to research, and incapable of sticking to a point. You are wandering very far from the consideration of the opera when you ask us to sympathize with the un-official status of the lusts of renegade clergy.'

Thomas clenched his fists, fully ready to attack Lightdown if Anna was once again prevented from reading her essay. But this time she stuck up for herself. 'Perhaps if I could just read a bit further?' she said.

'I shall fortify myself with some sherry, in that case,' said Alfie, getting up. 'Go, on, if you must, go on.'

So while Alfie fetches glasses, and pours from a decanter – three glasses, though his is the largest, and the only one more than half full – Anna reads on. Doggedly, and in a voice of monotonous level tone: 'A further problem in assessing the degree of obligation the betrothed couples were under, over and above the fact that we simply don't know if they were contracted to marry, or merely expecting to do so, when the opera opened, is the fact that there is no logical connection between the seriousness of an obligation and the seriousness with which one might have promised to undertake it in the future. One might frivolously, jokingly, promise that later one would take a solemn vow; as one might swear by all one held holy later to promise something frivolous.'

'Or, indeed, something impossible,' remarked Alfie, sitting down again. 'You cannot bind yourself to do the impossible, no matter how vehemently you promise.'

'But fidelity isn't impossible!' cried Thomas, protesting.

'This is Anna's essay,' said Alfie maliciously. 'What does she think?'

'I was trying to establish a distinction,' Anna said, looking up from her work, 'between the official obligations of a status like betrothal, or even marriage, which are general, and which change in different societies and different epochs without changing their rigid and generalized nature, and, on the other hand, obligations which are a matter of personal integrity – the promises, protestations and vows which we know the men have received before the opera opens, for it is on them that they base their confidence of their sweethearts' constancy. It is these private vows which, in the opera, ought to have bound the women, and do not.'

'Now, that's an interesting distinction, I agree,' said Alfie. 'And in these days in which people don't get engaged, or even, often, married, it makes a difference, doesn't it? Perhaps the right analogy, nowadays would be house purchase. Don't you agree, Thomas?'

'I don't quite get the bearing, sir.'

'Well, one puts one's house up for sale; one gets an offer, and one accepts it. Now, until the contracts are exchanged, one can change one's mind in outrageous ways. One can let the intended purchaser spend money on lawyers and surveyors, one can let them measure the rooms and spend fortunes on carpets, and so on, and then one can demand more money, change the price, or sell the house to another person, and the disappointed suitor has no comeback. He can only sue if you have breached a contract, not if you have broken a promise. And promise-breaking in this situation has become so commonplace it isn't even shocking; people will tell you that they did it for a thousand or so more, without blushing; otherwise respectable estate agents don't even raise their eyebrows at it. But the victim is always quite clear, that whether or not the law agrees, or society underwrites it, he has been done wrong. It's an interesting parallel, isn't it? Incidentally, I am old enough myself to remember a law against breach of promise to marry surviving on the statute books, though not often used . . . where were we?'

Anna resumed: 'it is these private vows which, in the opera, ought to bind the women, and do not. But in another of his typical devious tricks, Da Ponte has contrived to conceal from view the matching and corresponding vows which the men must have made in their turn, when wooing and winning the women. Those do not happen on stage; if they did we might notice, when the cross-paired wooing begins, that it involves the men in breaking their promises to their original partners. In being willing to pay court to another woman each of them has

119

broken already the faith that they are so indignant to find the women willing to break.'

Alfie heaved a huge sigh. 'Shooting the messenger again,' he said. 'Surely, my earnest young lady, you realize that the men woo only in fun; whereas the women are ready to marry the strangers and run off with them in earnest.'

'Whereas . . .' Anna read doggedly on, darting a resentful glance at Alfie as she went, 'there are many biological and economic reasons why sexual fidelity in men is of scant importance compared with the importance of it in women, it is hard to see how these excuses can apply at the level of personal faith, individual integrity, to which the discussion in the opera is so carefully confined. It would be fair to say, in fact, that the official thesis of the opera – that all women are unfaithful, Don Alfonso's theorem, which is demonstrated conclusively on stage – is supplemented by an unofficial one – Despina's theorem – which is that men are just the same:

> *Di pasta simile son tutti quanti;*
> *Le fronde mobile, l'aure inconstanti*
> *Han più degli uomini stabilità . . .*

(men are all made of the same stuff; the swaying boughs and changing breezes are more stable.) In fact a sour note infuses Despina's statement, giving her accusation a sharper edge than Don Alfonso's – "In us they love only their pleasure, then they despise us and deny us affection, and it is no use to ask for pity from the cruel ones." Despina's view, too, is conclusively demonstrated on stage. The resolution of the opera leaves any romantic belief in fidelity in ruins; it mounts, in fact, a devastating rationalist attack on romantic love, of which fidelity

120

is an essential foundation. For at the end the women return, humiliated and ashamed, to lovers who have shown themselves hypocritical, faithless and cruel; willing to inflict pain on their sweethearts in defence of foolish boasting, willing to evoke love fraudulently. Nobody can suppose this will make happy marriages; indeed we are told by Don Alfonso that the result will be husbands who are not deeply involved with their wives, who will remain within his sphere and do what he tells them. It is little wonder that *Cosi* has been so profoundly disliked.'

'But, Anna,' said Thomas, 'you realize there's nothing in the opera to support the idea that they return to their original partners at the end. Not a word. It has been produced successfully with them paired with the new lovers. For all we know that's what Mozart intended.'

'But from the point of view of the message, what difference would that make?' she said. 'We moderns tend to think they would be happier if they acted in the light of the knowledge that the "false" situation has revealed; but if so, then that's a good advertisement for falsity – one would be reading the opera as recommending shifting partners once a day on any whim . . . a worse thing even than Cressida, saying "to Diomede algate I wol be trewe" – at least she thought she ought to stop at Diomede!'

Thomas looked at Anna, appalled. He had been deeply impressed by the wonderful job she had been making of buttering up Alfie; he had expected at most one or two carefully planted disillusioned remarks, not a whole argued and articulated defence of rationalism. Alfie was obviously pleased. He had just refilled Anna's sherry glass, and now rubbed his hands gleefully, and said, 'Anna, we will make a cynic out of you yet! Perhaps I will forgo hearing

Thomas's essay this week; I have a feeling it would be relatively less uplifting.'

Thomas, seeing their chances slipping away, said, 'Sir, before we leave *Cosi*, I would be grateful if you could sum up for us.'

'What aspect of our far-ranging discussions needs summing up?'

'Well, if I have understood you correctly you think that the long unpopularity of the opera, its history of being neglected, or produced in mangled forms, is the result not of its really being a silly or immoral story, but of its containing an unwelcome truth, as outlined in Anna's essay. Have I got it right?'

'Perfectly. You can tell that there is something strange going on when you look at the vehemence with which *Cosi* has been attacked. In the nineteenth century it was attacked for immorality; Beethoven loathed it, and is said to have written *Fidelio* as a deliberate counter-blast, a counter-illustration of faithful female love. Not that loathing stopped him being influenced by it musically; remind me to mention that when we get to Beethoven. Wagner went even further; he was so convinced that it would have smirched Mozart's honour to write well to such a story that he contrived to convince himself that the music wasn't good, and that its failure to be good, in the circumstances, was a ground for admiring Mozart. And then various people edited the text; sometimes by having Despina spill the beans, so that the girls know that they are being fooled, and are simply acting along. Someone even took a Shakespeare play – was it *Love's Labour's Lost*? I can't remember – and rearranged the music as a setting of that . . . but all this condemnation contains, of course, an underlying assumption. You cannot think it immoral to write an opera about faithlessness in women if you think it is true that women are fickle.

122

More recently, of course, it is a charge of silliness that is made. If it is a very silly story, then there is no need to take any heed of its message. And that is odd too, when nearly every opera ever written is silly, if you insist on judging it so; is *Traviata* sensible, for example, or is *Bohème*?'

'And what is behind all this, you are saying, is an attempt to avoid confronting the message of the opera?' asked Thomas.

'Quite so. Because it projects one of the world's least popular universal truths. Very painful to learn, and best learned early.'

'Of course, if it's a universal truth, it should be possible – didn't you say? – to demonstrate it again?'

'Did I say that?' said Alfie, looking startled. 'Well, at least I might have said that if anybody was induced to take such a bet again the result would be the same.'

'That's what we have found confusing, sir,' said Anna. 'Since the disguises are so hard to believe in . . .'

'But you said you had found a way round that,' Thomas prompted.

'Well, supposing that the girls are not actually sisters,' said Alfie. 'They haven't seen each other's dear ones. They have a live-in job, let us say, which naturally, young females being what they are, makes them confide in each other.'

'But the moment the men turn up to woo, they will catch sight of each other!' said Anna.

'Ah. Picture to yourselves a house of many rooms, a garden of many bowers.'

'People don't usually have live-in jobs these days,' said Thomas.

'They don't live and die as servants in residence. But they might come for a while for special tasks . . . come, come, you have me wandering far from the point, and the allotted hour is up. Off with you now.'

Bundled abruptly on to the landing, Thomas and Anna started down the stairs.

'You were right, Anna, right!' cried Thomas, full of excitement. 'He really is doing it again! A country house somewhere; with some kind of work going on – cataloguing the books, repairing, replanting, that sort of thing!'

Anna did not answer him. 'All we have to do is find it . . .' His voice tailed away as he saw her unmoving, dejected face.

'Why bother?' she said. 'He's right, isn't he?'

'But you wanted . . .' A horrible thought struck Thomas. She wasn't acting. Her brilliant disillusioned essay was not what she had written to soften Alfie up for being pumped; it was what she really thought. Oh, no, Anna . . .

'But it's right. There's no such thing as true faith, true love. And so it doesn't matter where they are, or what he's doing to them. In that case nothing matters, Thomas.'

'Anna,' he said, taking her hand, and releasing it again when there was no response. 'Don't. Don't say that; come and talk to me; why didn't you come and talk to me?'

'Because nothing matters,' she said.

The rose garden is walled on three sides with mellow rose-gold bricks, rising to a stone coping, topped here and there with urns overflowing with lichen-blotched fruits. On the fourth side it is enclosed with a yew hedge, and a clipped archway opening on a long vista to the house. Set in the middle of the wall facing the vista, an elegant portico serves as a summerhouse, standing on a terrace with a little fountain. The rosebeds run round the walls, and along the yew hedge, and in an elaborate pattern cut into the pavement of the garden. The roses were once underplanted with herbs – lavender and creeping thyme and camomile – and the beds outlined in box and rue. Now weeds are rampant, the unpruned plants thickly entangled; the climbers have broken free under their own weight from the training wires, and fallen forwards prostrate; chaos, diamonded with a million sunlit beads of dew, spreads everywhere, but the roses bloom on in disarray, abundantly flowering, their collective perfume just discernible on the chill morning air. Overhead a sky faintly clouded, like opal or moonstone, promises unfiltered warmth and light at a later hour.

Dora comes into the garden carrying books. And waiting for her, leaning against a column of the portico, is a handsome fair young man, her adoring gardener. She ignores him, more or less, walking past him to set her books down on the rustic table within the summerhouse.

He sits down abruptly on a marble bench. 'I feel terrible,' he says. 'I might be dying.'

'You are back at work far too soon,' says Dora, looking at him coolly. 'Shock is always serious.'

'Your beauty is the graver shock,' he says. 'I'm dying for a kind word from you.'

'It's overactive shock,' says Dora. 'Sit down, and it'll wear off.'

'Ah, don't be unkind,' he says. 'Don't mock me.'

'I? Mock you?' she says. 'Would I? Look, I've brought us the lightest work in the garden, specially to go easy on you. All we have to do is list and identify the roses. You will sit here, shaded from the sun, and write down the names I call out to you, and look up the flowers I bring you.'

So she moves among the engulfed and tangled flowers and calls out their names to him. 'Rosa Turbinata, Apothecary's Rose, Rosa Mundi, Old Velvet Tuscany, Old Pink Moss, Great Double White, Celestial, Pompons des Princes . . . that one is called Isfahan, sometimes, I think . . . Rosa Ricardii, Rosa Moschata, Rosa Complicata, Old Blush China, Stanwell Perpetual, Gloire de Guilan – heavens, what a collection!'

Coming with handfuls of sample blooms to sit beside him, she says, 'Oh, but this is wonderful. I hadn't realized; I had glanced at it of course, and seen that there were some rarities; but so many really old stocks!'

'Do you like the old? Aren't new ones sweeter?'

'They are often bigger and brighter,' she says, 'but never smell so sweet. Now help me find what these are.'

Heads bent together they consult the dictionary of roses, comparing the delicate cut blooms with the hand-tinted botanical drawings, the long descriptions, the definitions of height and spread and provenance. The book is full of romantic details. Celestial, the only bush that bore scrolled blooms in the Middle Ages, loved by wicked Henry VIII; Great Maiden's Blush, known before the fifteenth century, widespread in monastery gardens; Isfahan, known for many centuries in Persia; Old Blush China, known before AD 900; Ricardii, the oldest rose of all, that King Minos might have plucked before ever young Theseus came – they have dozens to identify and enter on the roughly pencilled map of the flower beds. William is dazzled by the contrast between the long histories and the short lives of the gathered blooms, wilting in the rising heat of the day. The shade in which they sit deepens as the heat in the sunlit garden mounts, the dew burns off, the sky clears to azure, the garden hums with the industry of bees. By the time they finish, with Rosa Mutabilis and Belle Amour – detected by its pungent fragrance – he has his arm round her waist. He picks up the bloom of Rosa Mutabilis, and gives it to her, saying softly, 'This is for you.'

But as she takes it, he slips into the frail cup of its tender petals a little golden thing. 'Take it,' he says.

She extracts it from the petals, and studies it. A pendant. It bears a beautifully engraved design, of two roses. But the pair of swelling blooms, and their leaves and stems drawn together in a tiny ribbon, make a heart shape, have been applied to a golden heart.

'I can't let you give me a heart!' she says, withdrawing a little along the bench.

'It is only a token,' he says, smiling at her gently, 'a memento of the one you cannot stop me giving you, that yearns for you so painfully.'

She gets up, and goes to stand staring over the garden, her back to him. 'It seems to me positively cruel of you,' she says, 'to tempt me to break my word.'

'I can't help myself,' he says. 'I adore you. I am wholly yours. If I can't have what I want, I will want anything I can have, but I will never stop loving you. Please let me give you the pendant. Please take it. Don't you like it?'

'It's lovely,' she says. 'All right. I will keep it to remember you by. And thank you. But you know I am not free to make you any return.'

'A heart for a heart,' he says, 'would be fair exchange.'

The scent of the garden engulfs her. The warm air is balmy with it, and murmuring with the sound of ecstatic bees. So this is what it is like, she thinks, to be beautiful and young in a modern country; to be allowed to flirt, to receive flattery, to be entitled to be wooed . . .

'Ask all you like,' she says. 'My heart is not mine to give. My heart is far from here.' And in her thoughts a dark island looms out of an iron ocean, and her heart like a bird flies up the black sea-cliffs, and nestles against an imaginary Fernando, who stands on a rock ledge above a precipitous fall . . . she cannot recall his face. And while she thinks of him, the gardener comes up behind her, and puts his arms round her. He leans his head into the angle of her neck and shoulder, his left hand encircles her waist, and his right hand slips into her shirt, and presses over her left breast, the fingers warm and firm.

'What's this then?' he whispers to her. 'What's beating here?'

For a moment she leans into his embrace, and then twisting round she strikes him with a puny fist against his ribcage. 'I might as well ask you what's jumping around in there, if you've given your heart to me.'

'My true love hath my heart, and I have his,' he says. 'We must each have each other's. Let me put this where it longs to be . . .'

And he takes the pendant from between her fingers.

'I can't wear it,' she says.

'Close your eyes,' he tells her.

'What are you doing?'

'Don't look! . . . Now look . . .'

He has removed the chain on which she was wearing a locket, a present – but he couldn't know that – from Fernando, and deftly replaced it, but now the heart pendant hangs from it, and nestles against her.

'It suits you,' he says. 'Come and see.' He leads her

from the summerhouse to the edge of the basin of the clogged fountain. There in the still water the image of the two of them leans into the blue sky, and the little gold disc hanging from her neck catches the light and misses it, flickering like a bright fish in the depths.

'What could look better?' he says.

So this is what it is like, she thinks, to let a man adore you. To be loved at a whim, to be chosen freely, without restraint from friend or family or common sense. She had never expected to experience such delight, or – for it can come to nothing, must come to an early end – such poignant heartache.

'Don't go!' says Ferdy. 'You look at me as though I were a spider, or a snake or something; I only asked if we could walk together.'

Fleur does not stop, but moves swiftly along the gallery, leaving the cleaning behind her, and all her jars with the stoppers off. 'Shiv' walks at her shoulder, keeping up with her – but when he reaches out and lays a hand on her shoulder she shudders visibly.

'I see,' he says, halting abruptly. 'You really don't like me . . . am I so disgusting to you?'

'It isn't that,' she says. 'Not at all. But – you threaten my peace of mind.'

'I only want to make you happy.'

'Then leave me alone. Is that too much to ask?'

'But how can I bear to, when the last memory I shall carry with me is of you looking daggers at me, and running away? Couldn't you be just a little more gentle with me? I see you look at me, and an expression of hatred crosses your face . . .' He sounds really wounded. Fleur has stopped a pace or two ahead of him, and now looks round at him appalled. She is suddenly in doubt. Perhaps he isn't just fooling around?

'It gets worse and worse,' says Shiv. 'I see that you are sorry for me, and my love of you is confirmed. You are so tender, so gentle, you are made for kindness, incapable of cruelty . . . and I love and need you so much . . . won't you have pity on me?'

Fleur stands silent.

'I see not,' he says. 'I just hoped for a moment . . . You've no idea how painful it is to be shunned by someone one loves.' He walks away, down between the dust-sheeted chairs, into the darkened gallery.

As he goes she stretches out a hand to him, the word 'Wait,' on her lips, unuttered. But, no, let him go! she thinks. Every second I am with him I am in agony. I am longing to touch him, to hold him . . . I am horrified at myself. How can I feel like this? It serves me right if I am miserable, of course, it's a punishment for wicked desires. Oh, darling William, forgive me! But thinking about William forgiving her implies, of course, that he might come to know what she was feeling. God, no! Could one imagine telling a man who loves one that having once caught sight of another man naked one was constantly, caressingly undressing him in mind – that his presence burned one, like standing too near the fire? Secret, secret! Never to be told, to be stamped out of heart and mind, forgotten, buried . . . and so it will be, she resolves. She recalls William's unclouded smile, his candid expression, his charming, hesitant, hopeful avowal of love. Dearest William, she tells him silently, you deserved better of me.

'We could hire a car,' Thomas said, as he walked beside Anna. The water walks were blazing red and gold, the path lined with a rustling carpet of copper-orange hue, the brown water to left and right of them at the foot of the bank was flattening and darkening the leaf rafts which drifted on it. A robin sang with piercing sweetness overhead. Thomas with his arm through hers was leading Anna along, hoping somehow that the colours, like trumpets, like horns, would lift her heart, and break her gloomy mood.

Anna, her dark overcoat unbuttoned, her hands thrust in her pockets, walked looking down.

'We could hire a car, and drive around with a guidebook. We could go looking for a ruined stately home; there can't be that many. And one with no restoration or repair going on can be ruled out at once.'

'Thomas, hiring cars costs a fortune! And as you said, it might be only some cataloguing being done in the library, or something, and it would take hours to find out if anything is going on there. And he probably isn't doing it, anyway, and if he is it isn't any business of ours.'

'Anna, I don't understand you. Why don't you mind any more? You felt so angry for them, so eager to warn them; and I agreed. I liked you angry.'

Anna turned away, concealing her despondency, looking at a twig being swept away on the flow of the river. 'He likes me even less,' she thought.

'Where did you go? I tried to find you on Thursday. I wanted to tell you about *Love's Labour's Lost*. And you weren't there.'

'I went home for a night, that's all.'

'So what happened?'

'I just thought about things some more.'

'And thinking made you feel like this?'

'How can you know how I'm feeling?'

'Oh, Anna, easily! Please tell me about it.'

'It's just that it does seem to make life pointless. I

suppose I did hope to be happy in love, some day, with someone . . . but once you realize . . .'

'Anna, that vile old man is corrupting you! You mustn't let him, you mustn't! Just because some slimy youth has cheated him, it doesn't mean that everyone . . .'

'Well that is the very point under discussion, isn't it?' Anna said, bestirring herself to tackle Thomas. A bench occurred, and she sat down on it, legs thrust out in front of her. Two swans on the upper river, seeing them stop, turned towards them, showing mild interest. When they sat still the hope of bread vanished, and the swans turned away with dignity, their wings spread into the faint assistance of the barely perceptible fair wind.

'Thomas, if you knew that something was very difficult, you might try it; but if you knew it was impossible, you wouldn't, would you? Especially if it seemed likely you would get hurt in the attempt. If fidelity is impossible, that rules out trying love. I shall get used to the idea, I expect, but for the moment it's making me depressed. Sorry.'

'But Anna, all this discussion is just essays, you know. It's supposed to be teaching us about opera, not about life!'

'And do you really think this opera has nothing to teach us about life? Do you, Thomas?'

Thomas hesitated. But only for a moment. He took Anna seriously, and he realized that meant arguing honestly with her. The more it mattered the more damaging it would be to fail in candour.

'Well, of course art does matter,' he said. 'It carries all the messages we can hear from other times, all the experience there is to draw on. And opera is, can be, great art. But this one . . .'

'You're surely not going to tell me it's just a silly story, are you?'

132

'. . . is hard to understand. And Anna, if you think that somehow it rules out love, you simply have to be wrong. It contains the most beautiful arias, some of the most beautiful love songs ever written; it just can't be rubbishing love.'

'I think I'll tell you what happened when I went home.' The swans returned, just checking that there really would be no bread. They arched their necks at the same angle, at the same moment, and swam together like simultaneous notes on a stave.

'I thought, well, my mother and father have been married for years and years, and I think they are faithful; I can't imagine them not being. So, I thought, I'll go and ask my mother about it.'

'Christ, Anna! What a thing to do!' he said.

'Why? Why shouldn't I?'

'Well, what if the true answer was that your parents have five lovers apiece? What if the truth was that they are horribly unhappy, would you want to be told? Would your mother want to be asked?'

'I didn't think of that,' said Anna, sadly. 'How crass of me.'

'Well, was the answer like that?' Thomas asked. 'Is that what's upset you?'

'No, not exactly. She said she was happy. She said she had been faithful all the time, and Daddy had been nearly all the time. "Nearly" surprised me a bit, but the rest is what I thought she would say. They always seemed very jolly together, and given to laughing just out of earshot of everyone; you know.'

'Well then, what?'

'Her face lit up, Thomas, and she said, "Of course, when I first knew your father my knees used to go watery whenever he came into the room." You should have seen how she smiled, saying that. So I said, "But that doesn't happen now?" And she just laughed. So I said, "But didn't you promise to love

133

each other for ever and ever?" And she said, "Oh, Anna, you chump, one can't promise that one's knees will wobble for the rest of one's life!"'

'Well, no,' said Thomas. 'I can see that.'

'So I said, "Well, what do you do when they stop wobbling? There you are, having promised enormous things, and you just don't feel like it any more. What do you do?" And she said that you pretend.'

'*Did* she?' Thomas sounded surprised. 'That doesn't sound right. Are you sure that's what she said?'

'Well, not in so many words, but that's what it amounted to. She said you can't help how you feel, but you can help what you do and say. She said you keep your promise by going on "acting lovingly" however you feel. So I said I didn't think much of acting with the person in the whole world you are supposed to feel closest to. And then it sort of came out, as we were talking, that we didn't at all mean the same thing by "loving". What I meant was the flow of feeling, as natural as a river, that you felt without constraint, in your secretest inner self. What she meant by it was always being kind, saying nice things, remembering birthdays, whether you feel like it or not. And there's worst to come, Thomas. I thought her kind of loving was dreadful; a kind of deep-dyed hypocrisy, and she thought mine was just silly, whimsy stuff. She said it wouldn't do to base a life on. So there we are.'

'Yes. Well, where are we exactly, Anna? And this is why you are depressed?'

'Well, it's pretty dire, isn't it?'

'The nub of the matter being?'

'That mother, who is faithful, and says she is happy, agrees with that loathsome turd, Mr Lightdown, that love is impossible.'

'But that isn't what she said.'

'It's what she meant. What it amounted to.'

'Are you absolutely sure, Anna,' asked Thomas, uncomfortably aware that his own parents, and even the graduate student couple, married three months, with whom he had lodged in the vacation, were getting by quite smoothly on what Anna called deep hypocrisy, 'are you sure that acting lovingly would be so bad?'

'Well, think it through. Let's suppose you love someone . . .'

Flinching inwardly, Thomas supposes so.

'. . . and suddenly you realize that they don't actually feel like being with you that afternoon; that they don't actually feel like making love to you, but that, so as not to hurt your feelings, they are pretending. What then?'

'I'd be pretty upset. It would hurt.'

'But would you accept it? Would you accept the pretended affection, or let them force themselves to make love to you?'

'No. If she was forcing herself to stay, I'd open the door for her, and say goodbye.'

'And the more deeply you loved someone the less you would want them to "act lovingly"; the more you would want them to go the moment they felt like it. It's true, Thomas, isn't it?'

'Yes, it is,' he said. For it was.

'So now you see how depressing it is. What we really want from each other, what lovers want, is to be the object of involuntary desire, to be loved with love like a flowing river, freely, naturally. But people can't control how they feel. As mother says, you can't promise to have wobbly knees in thirty years' time – or even next week, come to that. The only thing you could promise – to control your conduct, to behave yourself lovingly – the other person would not want. They wouldn't want love if they thought it came about from trying, from deliberate control. You can reasonably promise what lies within your power to control; but when you promise to love someone you promise what nobody can be sure of being able to do.'

'So the marriage vow ought really to be, "I promise always to behave myself as if I loved you."'

'And that has nothing to do with what people mean by love. People could promise that, and keep the promise, too, who didn't love each other, didn't even like each other, didn't even know each other at all.'

'No, Anna, I don't think they could. People's capacity for pretending isn't that great. If it was just an act, it would be a bad one.' A man, he thought, might have particular difficulties pretending desire if he didn't feel it.

'Worse and worse,' she said. There was a gloss on her cheek, so that he wondered if she was crying again; they had talked into the shortening daylight, and in the creeping onset of dusk he couldn't quite see.

'We'd best walk back,' he said. 'They lock the gate at sunset.'

They strolled back. The swans resisted nightfall, glowing against the sombre shades of bank and dark river.

'It must happen sometimes that people's feelings continue unchanged all their lives,' he said. 'There must be some people with wobbly knees after years and years. It isn't wholly impossible, Anna, it must have happened in the history of the world. So we could hope for it.'

'You could hope to discover nuclear fusion, or live to a hundred and eighty,' she said, shrugging. 'There's a lot of the history of the world.'

They walked in silence for a while.

'All right, then,' he said. 'Faithful love is a very remote possibility. We had better make a distinction between love and fidelity, or love itself looks chancy.'

'We can't,' she said. 'They are hopelessly tangled together. What's the first thing you say when you fall in love? Everyone does. "I'll love you forever . . . till all the seas run dry, my dear . . . if this be error and upon me proved . . ." everyone.'

'Would it help if they didn't?' Thomas wondered aloud.

'Not much. Do you remember that scandal last term, when someone dropped a girl he had been living with just before finals? He kept saying he hadn't promised her anything. But because he was living with her, everyone, including her, assumed that he had. In effect. Loving someone constitutes promising to go on. It's inescapable.'

'So what conclusion are you coming to, Anna? Where does this argument lead?'

'Those exceedingly unfashionable Christian thinkers who approve of celibacy may have a point. If one wanted to keep one's honour and truth, one would have to avoid love.'

'But, Anna, Anna dearest,' he said, – they had reached the wrought iron gates that divided the water walks from the rest of the gardens, and just in time, for the porter was standing there, rattling his keys – 'couldn't one then just love someone, and never let a promise cross one's lips?'

'But loving someone implies the promise that one cannot know one can keep,' she said, as they turned under the arches into the quadrangle. 'I suppose implied promises are easier to disown than overt ones. Of course they are. So I do think one should avoid making overt ones. I shall resolve never to promise anything. But you can't, Thomas, can you? It's too late for you!'

Whereupon, throwing in his direction a glance that he could not read in the gloom of the unlit cloisters, she quickened her pace, and ran away towards the gates.

And Thomas felt as though his soul had been beaten and bruised. He felt battered by the conversation. And shamed; found wanting by it, as though he had watched a friend drowning, and failed to draw them to dry land. It seemed to him that he had got to find an answer to Anna's despair. Even if he was not the one to benefit – it didn't seem likely to him that he would be the man whom Anna came to love – for her sake he must somehow convince her to find courage, to be ready to take risks.

'What has happened ever, even once in the history of the world, can happen again,' he thought. And then, burning with love and desire, he said aloud to the empty quadrangle, the golden windows, the shadowy tower against the first faint stars, '*Eppur' si muove!* I *will* love her for ever!'

William walks through an overgrown avenue, making his way to the meeting point, and sunk in misery as he goes. He had somehow, in the pleasure and delight of courting Dora in the rose-garden, managed to overlook the inevitable consequence of success – that he would have to confront Ferdy and tell him what had happened. 'And how would I feel,' he wonders, 'if Ferdy had any such news to bring me? Not that he could have . . .' For William honestly trusts and believes in his Fleur. But he would be devastated, thrown into the utmost misery, if Ferdy did manage to sway her, and this is the catastrophe that his little rôle-playing in the rose garden will inflict on his friend. And William is fond of Ferdy, genuinely, rather admires him for his wonderful panache and robust good cheer and strange, old-fashioned, fluent English, which makes conversation with him feel like being in a play, feel stylish and witty.

Some of the glamour of the east shines about Ferdy, and rubs off on William. William, an eldest child and only son, with a bevy of adoring sisters, and the admiration of his schoolteachers, who did not often get a pupil into Oxford, has always been rather full of himself for everybody's taste. But from the first, instead of being affronted by him, Ferdy had laughed. Ferdy had assumed that William's bumptiousness was a deliberate form of foolery, intended to amuse. His laughter had educated William, pulled him into shape, taught him that more refined form of self-assertion that takes the form of modesty. William, who is not apt to look up to people, does admire Ferdy. And what a way to pay a debt! He plods on, through the kitchen gardens, feeling as he used to feel when going to the dentist, or as he felt that time he had to own up to breaking a window . . . an appropriate objective correlative of misery, that thought, because the assignation with Ferdy and Alfie is to take place in the greenhouse, and coming within sight of it he sees at once that it has dozens of broken panes.

And bursting out of it at every point, reaching frantic fingers towards the light – those panes that are intact are filthy – is a riotous grapevine, bearing by the hundred little green bunches of potential grapes. Its exuberance reminds William of what he is trying not to feel, the little scandalous singing note of joy, audible through all the respectable heavy feelings, the wicked joy that he has Dora like a bird in the hand . . .

Ferdy is sitting on a rusty Victorian garden seat,

139

under the canopy of vine. A dim green light filtered through occluded glass and freshly verdant leaves gives him an underwater appearance. Alfie has not yet arrived. And Ferdy greets him, smiling, with, 'Didn't I tell you we'd win?'

William stands looking down at his friend – the lean, handsome face, fine dark eyes, the slender form draped gracefully across the rigid chair, the expensive casual silk shirt, open at the neck just enough to show the glint of a heavy gold chain – and William is unable to control himself, swept away on a gust of reprehensible feeling, his inner self sounding trumpet-peals of joy – see, my rich and handsome friend, both women love *me*! – while he tries hard to maintain a suitably sombre expression.

'I couldn't get anywhere with her,' says Ferdy. 'She just sent me packing. Rather humiliating, actually. But you must have found it so, too.'

Silently William sits down, and puts on the intricate little iron table between them the golden locket he had so cunningly lifted from round Dora's neck.

Into the silence he says, uneasily, 'One should perhaps always be a little untrusting, in this hard world.'

'She gave you that?' says Ferdy, speaking slowly.

'Not exactly,' says William, casting about desperately for a gentle way to put it. 'She let me take it.'

And he is horrified to see that tears have sprung into Ferdy's eyes. 'The bitch! The judas!' Ferdy says. '*I* gave her that.' And he sweeps it contemptuously off the table, so that it falls at William's feet, and springs open, revealing a tiny portrait of Ferdy.

Ferdy gets up, and begins to blunder along the greenhouse towards the door.

'Where are you going?' says William in alarm, going after him. 'Come back!'

'I'm going to find her and kill her!' says Ferdy. William, restraining him, finds him trembling from top to toe with rage.

'No, you're not, Ferdy. Do you want to serve life for a jilt? Calm down. Just sit here with me for a while, and give yourself time to think.'

Ferdy rummages frantically in the pocket of his jacket, and brings out his silver-mounted hip flask, and swigs at it. When he offers it to William, William shakes his head.

Ferdy's rage is subsiding into misery, deeply up-setting William, who has seen him angry before, but never seen him despairing. 'Oh God!' says Ferdy. 'All those innocent, shy smiles, and promises, and little tender words and touches . . . how can the wicked girl forget them so soon?'

'I don't know,' says William. 'It's amazing; but . . .'

'But? But what?'

'But I suppose we have been warned. I mean women have a reputation for it, don't they? If you read poetry you find all those complaints – "a bitter fashion of forsaking" endlessly bewailed . . . it's happened before. I mean if we believe what we read, women have deceived hundreds and thousands of men.' He looks disconcerted as a light breeze blows a scutter of dry leaves and dust across the flagstones of the floor, as though the ghosts of dead lovers stirred at his words.

'What shall I do?' says Ferdy, softly. 'Help me, William. Give me some advice.'

'I don't know what to say,' says William.

'You don't know what a fool you have made of me,' says Ferdy bitterly. 'Alfie will laugh himself silly, of course; how he will laugh at my stupidity! But so will my grandmother, and my uncles and my aunt . . .'

141

'But . . . need you tell everyone?' asks William, baffled.

'I'll have to give some explanation. It makes me sick to think of it! If you knew how high and mighty I have been over their opinions, how I have mocked and derided them, and told them they are just down from the trees, for thinking that any girl with western ways would be a harlot! No, no, I have told them, they don't understand, western girls go about freely, and choose their own companions, and this is nothing but a different, and, I have told them, a better, convention, and such girls are perfectly chaste and loyal, and indeed, safer because they know how to withstand temptation . . . and all the while my whole family is telling me that all women are hot for sex all the time, and incapable of resisting any and every seducer, and that is why they must be chaperoned, and watched, and kept behind locked doors . . . God, how they will laugh at me!'

'But do you have to tell them?'

'When I throw her over I will have to say why.'

'But do you have to throw her over, just for a locket?' cries William, in mounting alarm. 'You make it seem like Desdemona's fucking handkerchief!'

And now Ferdy is looking at him white-faced, tight-lipped. 'I can't possibly marry a girl who might not be a virgin!' he says.

'Bloody hell, Ferdy! Hang about! Who says she isn't a virgin? I certainly haven't been any further than I have told you.'

'Bloody hell, William!' says Ferdy, almost weeping, 'If you can get so far so soon, who can tell what someone else might have managed?'

'Christ!' says William. 'I knew we shouldn't have got into this. But Ferdy, it doesn't follow, really it doesn't, that just because I could . . .' He breaks off.

Actually he feels perfectly sure that Dora is virtuous; it doesn't seem at all likely to him that because he has managed to wheedle the locket from her, and fix to take her out tonight, any other man could have fooled about with her. He attributes his success to his own potent attractions, to his own charm and cunning . . . women have always liked him . . . but he is thinking better of putting this explanation to Ferdy.

When Ferdy says fiercely 'Push off!' William goes.

'It'll be a good revenge, of course,' Ferdy tells himself, desolately. 'All I have to do is disown her, and she'll never get another Indian bridegroom. She'll be disgraced. All I have to do is disown her, and forget her – stamp her out of heart and mind.' But he does have overmuch self-knowledge for that project.

'Oh, but I can't!' he cries. 'Whatever she has done, however she has treated me, I adore her! I think I know it more clearly than before. I will love her for ever and ever, and if I stopped I would die!'

Thomas strode through the misty streets. Oxford was wrapped in indigo tissue, the exhalation of its rivers and the onset of night. Lamps were blurred and magnified by the atmosphere into soft spreading smudges of dull gold, with no sharpness in them. He had buttoned his mackintosh to the chin, and having forgotten to grab his scarf as he dashed out on his errand, was walking with his shoulders hunched to close the gap between collar and neck. He was making for Anna's room, and bracing himself as he went to be repelled, misunderstood, when he got there. He had not presented himself at her door since the afternoon of the punk disguise, whose effects had so disastrously compromised him. He had no right to expect to be taken for a safe and respectable visitor, but he did have to see Anna at once. The present he had bought for her – slipping into the shop just before it closed, after she had left him that afternoon – jutted awkwardly from his pocket.

Anna's hostel was a little distance from the centre, and he walked in tree-lined streets with darkness between the pools of lamplight. Looking up as he neared the building he saw that the mist was barely thick enough to keep him out of his depth in it; above him clear and brilliant was a black sky full of stars. There in their timeless glory were the Plough and the Bear and the Pleiades, and he could see them a million miles away, though he could not see more than a yard or two ahead.

At Anna's door he knocked and went in without waiting. She was sitting in front of her gas fire, in her only chair: thinking, he supposed, for she wasn't reading. She did seem surprised to see him, though not, as he had thought possible, alarmed.

'You are too late,' she said, 'I've just eaten the last biscuit.'

'I didn't come for food,' he said, taking off his coat and, noticing that it was lightly beaded with dew, dropping it on the floor instead of putting it on her bed. He sat down and held his hands to the red-hot ceramic waffles of the elderly gas fire. As he did so there was a triumphant click from the meter, and the fire went out.

'I told you you were too late,' she said. 'I haven't any money till I go out tomorrow. I'll have to go to bed to keep warm.' Biting back an imperative urge to offer to go with her, and double the thermal output in the bedclothes, Thomas said, 'I've got a fifty,' and produced one from his pocket.

144

Anna found a match, and they relit the fire. 'Anna, how well do you know *Cosi*?' he said. 'The music, I mean.'

'I've seen it done on television,' she said. 'And I heard a concert performance of it. Both a while back. Why do you ask?'

'Well, I've said to you twice, I think, "Listen to the music," and you haven't responded. I just wondered.'

'I've been referring to the score for working on it with Lightdown,' she said.

'There's a lot of difference between reading music and listening to it,' he said. 'And there's a lot of difference between what Da Ponte thought and what Mozart thought. And what Da Ponte thought doesn't matter a bent pin except because of Mozart.'

'I don't get you,' said Anna.

'I know you don't. There's what the English buffs call a subtext in the music. And I want you to listen to it. So I brought you this. It's a present.'

He took from his overcoat pocket the damp paper bag, containing a boxed set of tapes of *Cosi fan Tutte*, and laid it on her lap.

'Oh, but Thomas! I can't let you do this; whatever did this cost?' she said.

'It's with love, Anna. Just listen to it,' said Thomas, jumping up, seizing his coat and departing before he did something silly.

When Alfie appears in the greenhouse, Ferdy snarls at him, 'Go away!'

'Charming!' says Alfie. 'What manners!'

'You are cold and cruel and ruthless,' says Ferdy. 'You cause misery. And then you talk of manners? Go away!'

Alfie sits down. 'So Fleur is faithful, and Dora, it seems, not,' he says.

'I am bitterly ashamed,' says Ferdy.

'William obviously thinks this result is the effect of the superior force of his kind of attachment,' says Alfie. 'He tells me that after all, one would not expect a young woman arranged into an engagement to feel as deeply and sincerely as a young woman who has fallen freely in love with someone, western style. Do you accept that?'

Ferdy looks up, giving up on the attempt to hide his tears, and sees Alfie staring at him, bright-eyed, head cocked to one side. For a moment he feels like a corpse under the eye of a scavenging crow.

'William is also enquiring if I will pay up to just one of you, if one wins, and the other loses the bet.'

Ferdy makes no reply.

'But I think before paying him, we should have one more try, don't you? He just might be counting chickens. So buck up, man; go and wash your face, and then go and find the supposed Penelope, and try what happens if . . .'

So they leave the green shade of the vine, and walk together towards the house. They enter together by the neglected door at the foot of the turret, together climb the stair into the turret rooms on the opposite corner of the house from that used by the girls. At the door of the room which had served as his sick room Ferdy parts from Alfie, and goes to wash his burning face and change his shirt. Why grief should crumple shirts is not clear to him, but he feels the need to cast off every stitch he was wearing in the greenhouse, and start clean and different.

Alfie climbs on, and enters on the next floor a room with a fire lit in a shining grate, flowers in Delft vases on polished furniture, faded glowing rugs, everything bright and inviting. A belvedere window gives a wide prospect of the ruined garden, and even of the outside world, for a swelling curve of hillside clothed in wheatfield can be seen, and behind it the tower of a village church. In the bed in this room a man is lying like a great fallen tree. On a little table at the head of the bed the impedimenta of nursing are cluttered on a clean cloth.

'I seem to see a lot of you these days,' the sick man says. 'Are you going to tell me what's going on?'

Hearing voices, the nurse steps in from the next room, her own sitting room, where she is very comfortable – hers is a good job, though lonely – and seeing Alfie she tactfully withdraws and closes the door. She cannot make out the tenor of Alfie's voice, spinning some tale or other to her patient. She hopes it is something cheerful, being very fond of her patient, who is a strikingly handsome man, and seldom sharp with her.

His voice, however, is more penetrating, or perhaps just more familiar to her. She hears him say, 'Oh, for God's sake, Alfie, why not just leave them alone?' And then she withdraws from earshot, since she suspects, but does not choose to know, why her employer, who seems not to be a relation, lavishes care on the patient, and insists that he wants for nothing.

'Why, my dear,' Alfie is saying, 'do you object to people heading for disaster having fair warning?'

'How can you be sure they would be heading for disaster if you left well alone?'

'Easy. If someone like you, Roland, could not be faithful to someone like me, then nobody can be faithful to anybody.'

'Rubbish, Alfie. There's nothing special about me – or you.'

'Evidently you thought so. When I remember the

number of my rivals, and their average level of refinement . . . only your illness put a stop to it, and delivered you into my hands.'

'It would be easier to bear your kindness if it were accompanied by some forgiveness for the past.'

'How can I forgive you without ceasing to love you?' says Alfie, standing with his back to the room, looking out of the window.

'You may imagine, if you will, how I detest your fidelity!' came the reply. 'But doesn't it rather disprove your own thesis? And even if it doesn't, Alfie, you have got everything wrong. Of course the young are deluded; driven headlong by that old bitch nature; but it doesn't follow it would be better if they weren't. There's a season for knowing the truth, Alfie, and it isn't youth. You debauch them, trying to make them cynical before their time. The world would come to an end if the young became self-preserving. You are trying to stop the world.'

'Well, before it stops, is there anything in the world I can bring for you? Anything in the world I can do?'

'Get out of here. And leave the babes in the wood alone. Learn to hate in ordinary ways like everybody else. You'll feel better for it.'

'You should know,' says Alfie, leaving.

Anna played *Cosi* to herself. She put on earphones, and shut out the outer world, and let the music flow into her. And as she listened, she began to wonder urgently about Mozart. What can he have been like? Was he really like the creature in *Amadeus*, which she saw last year in the cinema? Of course, she remembered, what Peter Shaffer was offering was not what he himself thought Mozart was like, but what he thought Salieri would have thought. Outside Salieri's jealous and fevered mind could there really have been such dissonance between a man's talent and a man? Perhaps there could. But where would that leave the idea that Thomas seemed to propose, that one might let the subtext, Mozart's music, form one's opinion about love? Could that be a valid thing to do if Mozart was really crude, vulgar, debauched, spendthrift, foul-mouthed?

Anna, frantic to know more about him, raced down to the college library, just before it closed for the night, and seized all she could find about Wolfgang Amadeus. Alfie's card, arriving the next morning, requesting an essay on 'The Life', came *à propos*, since it found her already working on it.

'In one way, of course,' she wrote, 'a lot is known about Mozart. There are volumes of his letters, passages describing him in the memoirs of others, biography and commentary, a plethora of volumes. Even his childhood is documented and recorded, for he seemed phenomenal from the beginning. "The miracle which God permitted to be born at Salzburg," and these words are his father's, is the only composer who evokes such feelings of reverence approaching idolatry. "The divine Mozart" runs easily off the tongue, off the pen of writers, and sounds more conformable with truth, less challenging than even "The divine Beethoven" does. Whereas "The divine Verdi, the divine Wagner, the divine Bizet," just sound silly. And from the beginning the divine figure is deeply ambivalent, and those who tell us about him can seldom command even a semblance of objectivity. His father who taught him and fostered his talent also took him about Europe at a tender age like a performing monkey, and let idiots subject his talents to tests at the keyboard. A solemn fellow in London offered a report on the boy, then aged eight, to the Royal Society – a phenomenon! – and mentioned his compositions of love and rage in operatic style. How odd, how odd, that Mozart's first symphonies were probably written in a London suburb! How touching that so many of the stuffed owls of the age who flocked to him to be dumbfounded, not by his talent, but by his possessing it so young, also liked him: "*une des plus amables créatures qu'on puisse voir*," licensed to jump into the lap of an empress, and demand a kiss.

'But how difficult it is to discern in all this an impression of what he was really like. There is, of course, a well-established Mozart legend. According to this he was exploited in his childhood by a cold, ambitious, place-seeking and subservient father, who never forgave him for breaking free in adult life. He earned a little brief worldly glory, not much of it in his own city, never held a major appointment, and was scorned – kicked in the arse, even – by his employer. His emperor tolerated but never advanced him. The woman he loved rejected him, and he was tricked into marrying her sister, who was a selfish slut. The Viennese got tired of him, and preferred the music of nonentities: he fell into poverty and died in misery, probably poisoned by a jealous rival. He was given a pauper's burial, thrown into quicklime in an unmarked grave, and nobody followed his coffin to its final rest. When he died he was working on a Requiem, commissioned by a mysterious stranger, which he believed was for himself.

'This, of course, makes of Mozart a martyr, certainly divine – a light shining in the darkness, which comprehended it not. But it is, of course, a legend; in which nearly every element is questionable.

'We might prefer another Mozart, the affectionate, joking boy, signing himself "Jack-pudding" on letters home, asking his sister about the pet canary, owing everything to his father's recognition and fostering of his talent. This Mozart never learned worldly wisdom, and was tricked into marriage with a nondescript girl (no version has any sympathy for Constanze!), but he led a life full of fun, carousing with friends, playing billiards, wasting his money, with music pouring out of him effortlessly on to clean, uncorrected pages: super-human, divine! He died suddenly, just as his reputation was about to bring wealth and invitations from abroad, and when the Viennese were once more flocking to hear his music, in Schikaneder's pantomime production of *The Magic Flute*. Whatever infection the doctors of his time called by the name "miliary fever", it was that which carried him off. His household was not unusually strapped for money when he died, and he was buried in the usual way for a middle-class Viennese, indeed exactly in accordance with the method of burial laid down by the meticulous authoritarian emperor; among those who followed the coffin to the city gates – it was not usual for mourners to go further – was the man accused by posterity of having poisoned him: Salieri, who seems to have admired him. He never lacked for admiration, and his greatest contemporary, Haydn, paid him lavish tribute in many quarters.

'Or should we prefer a Mozart who started life optimistic, cheerful, candid and naïve, who knew how good he was and innocently supposed that the world would gladly acknowledge him and find him an honorable sustenance, and who gradually, bruised by a thousand rejections, condescensions, humiliations and insults, became disgusted with the world and withdrew from it, writing ever more magnificent and less appreciated works – "too many notes, tough meat for my Viennese," as the emperor said – and eventually, cast off by all good society and reduced to begging, must have welcomed death, unresisting?'

In each book that Anna picked up the outline of Mozart was different. Was it simply that he was all these men, that all these pictures would have seemed nearly right to those who knew him? Padding barefoot along the corridor to the gas rings to make coffee to keep herself awake, Anna thought about it. She felt a clear sense of unease, very like the unease which struck when she was thinking about *Cosi*, a sense that something living and ebullient was being chopped to fit. Somehow everybody seemed shocked at something about Mozart. Because we adore his music, Anna thought, we read his letters, take issue with his language, express embarrassment at his love talk, disapprove of his choice of wife, wince at his requests for money . . . because we think of him as divine we patronize him off the face of the earth, and at the same time execrate the stupid patricians of his day who patronized him on it.

Carrying her coffee back to her room she continued writing: '. . . People have so hated being reminded that their deity was a man with the usual bodily functions that his letters, full of jokes about shit, have remained unpublished, or seen the light only heavily censored. The twentieth century takes the anal fixation (but Mozart thought shit was funny, not serious) in its stride, but reads appalled his letter on the death of his father, and accuses him of mercenary coldness. Protestant writers ignore or minimize his Catholic piety, and imply that any religious belief less forceful than Bach's is too frivolous to count for much, though Mozart himself

152

claimed to feel religion deeply, and instanced "*Agnus Dei, qui tollis peccata mundi . . .*" as the sort of text which moved him. Meanwhile Catholic writers are appalled at his Freemasonry. Everyone agrees in deploring his wife, and believing that Mozart was entrapped into marriage with her. On this matter the opinion of Leopold Mozart, in a haughty, icy and angry letter to his son, a letter which must have given irreparable pain, is the view which has prevailed. But however low, vulgar, unmusical, sluttish and faithless Constanze was, Mozart seems to have loved her. Of course he loved her; his letters are full of affection and concern. What shines clear from his letters to his silent wife (not a word of any letter of hers to him survives) is his confident expectation of enjoying himself in her company when they are next together. Even his reproaches speak of love. Reading a love letter to her in which he describes unfastening his flies and playing with his cock as he thinks of her, longs for her, one may smile, as the commentators hardly know which is worse, the lewdness or the object of it. But it was written for Constanze, not for nineteenth- and twentieth-century stuffed owls, and Constanze probably liked it.

'Who on the other hand, could read without pain and shame the letter he wrote to Michael Puchberg, on whom in his darkest times he relied for money – "You are right, dearest friend, not to honour me with a reply. My importunity is too great . . ." Would Puchberg have been more generous if he had known that his only ticket to immortality, his only claim to any attention from the future, would be as a friend of Mozart's? Probably not. Probably he was already as generous as he could afford to be.'

Anna was getting tired. She could not possibly write more, and indeed had no sensible need to be writing in the small hours since the tutorial was not the next morning. An owl hooted in the moonlight outside. She got up and went to look out through her uncurtained window. And she could see only through her own shadowy outline, which masked the reflections of the room behind her, dimly bright in the light of her desk lamp. But through her shadow self she saw the sailing dusky white kite of the bird glide from tree to tree, bent on murder.

Anna collapsed in her chair. She was too tired to continue, and her mind was too busy to allow her at once to sleep. Her coffee was untouched, and cold. She wondered if she herself would have liked Mozart.

Late in his life Mozart put out a subscription list, offering exclusive use of new compositions to those who put down their names. He collected just one name. Whose name was it? she wondered. Was it known whose it was? She would look it up in the morning. Obviously all the later writers whom Anna had been feverishly reading thought that they themselves would have recognized Mozart; thought that those who did not were philistine fools. Would I have put down my name? Anna asked herself. And knew at once that if the name was put down from true recognition, in the midst of life and without hindsight, of music genius, then the name would never have been hers; but if it was put down by some fool out of kindness, then it might have been. As she fell asleep, still dressed and sitting in the chair, she had one of those glimpses of the obvious that linger on the margins of sleep, and dazzle us with a false appearance of brilliance. None of this matters, she told herself. Nothing matters about Mozart except the sound of his music. Outside her window a mortal wail sounded as the owl found its aim, but she did not hear it.

*   *   *

Dora is sitting comfortably in the kitchen, perched
on a tall stool, with her legs locked round the stool
legs, watching Roz prepare lunch, and nibbling off-
cuts of vegetables, dipping fingers in the sauces and
licking them. On being asked she begins to cut
slivers of cheese with a wire cutter. The room is full
of the wonderful smells of baking bread and
crushed garlic, and full also of the immemorial
companionship of women sharing domestic tasks,
the immemorial context for confidences, secrets,
talk about men.

'Now you sound like a grown-up woman!' Roz is
saying, smiling at Dora.

'I certainly shouldn't have let him wheedle away
my locket,' Dora says. 'I'll have to make him give it
back. But that young devil is so sweet-talking, so
tricky, you'd need a heart of stone to resist him. I did
try; really I did!'

'You're in luck, Dora, luckier than you know,' Roz
says. 'A cunning and fluent lover! Wonderful; there
aren't very many like that. Mostly they're bumbling,
clumsy and shy. There isn't much classy affection in
the world, my dear; we must find it where we can.'

She breaks off as Fleur arrives, clattering down
the stairs, and throws herself into the crooked
Windsor chair at the head of the kitchen table. She
has been crying; her eyes are swollen and red.

'Why, what's happened to upset you?' asks Roz,
going at once to put a kettle on the stove.

'What's the trouble?' says Dora, reaching out for
Fleur's hand.

'You are!' cried Fleur. 'May I, you, Roz, Shiv, the
owner, and every other crazed wrecker the world
contains rot in hell!'

'Why, what have we done?' says Roz. 'Do you want a cup of tea?'

'You've talked me into my own misery,' says Fleur. 'I'm in love; and not with William.'

'Hurrah,' says Roz.

'You too!' says Dora, smiling.

'Good for you; why not?' says Roz.

Dora turns over Fleur's hand which lies limply in hers, and looks intently at the lines on it. 'Follow your heart, dear friend,' she says. 'Like me, you are to be happy.'

'How can you say that?' Fleur demands, straightening in her chair. 'What about the pain we will inflict on our fiancés? What about that? They love us truly – think how they will suffer when they come back! Where did you learn such callousness? What has made you so unlike your old self?'

'My old self?' says Dora. 'But what about my true self? I am out from under my family's eyes for the first time, and just learning who I am! I have learned from watching western girls, and reading western books. I am going to flirt, and enjoy myself, and take my chances, and only when I must am I going to choose the one I prefer. And you should do the same. When, and if, the others come back, will be soon enough to worry about them. If our hearts have been won away in the meantime we shan't sit around to be reproached – we'll be off and away!'

Fleur listens in silence. 'But I'm afraid,' she says. 'Aren't you afraid to discover how swiftly such strong feelings can change? How can we be so altered? How can we live, knowing that any minute we may feel differently?'

'What a silly question,' says Dora. 'We're only human, and nothing human is for ever. Did you think it was? Have you told your new fellow you are falling for him?'

156

'Certainly not. I sent him packing. I can control myself.'

'That won't last long,' says Roz. 'Shall we have lunch here, since here's where we are, and it's ready?'

'You'll see,' says Fleur. 'And I'm not hungry.'

'Believe me,' says Dora to Fleur, 'you'd do better to give in. Why struggle against love? Love is a sneak, a thief, who filches your peace of mind as he likes. As soon as an image of someone gets to your innermost heart, you've lost your liberty. Love isn't voluntary – is it? Would you feel as you do if it were? There's joy and delight in following your inclination, and nothing but misery and disgust if you fight against it.'

'But if we behaved like that, how we should be condemned! We wouldn't have a shred of reputation left!'

'I'll tell you something about that,' says Roz. 'Something I've noticed about people who condemn – who disapprove of sex outside marriage and adultery within it, of broken engagements and holiday romances, who hold by the whole book of words – such people are always those who have been dealt a lucky hand of cards, and are in a position to secure their own happiness without breaking the rules. You could count on the fingers of one hand all those in the whole wide world who have upheld the rules to their own detriment. Really. The opinions of the rule-keepers are only luck and selfishness unpleasantly combined with bullying. They have no moral standing. You should take no notice.'

'Do what you want to do,' says Dora, speaking laughing, bright with joy. 'I'm going to!'

*   *   *

Thomas walked on Port Meadow, thinking about Anna. It was bitterly cold and still, frost-splintered grass cracked under his feet, and the air, glass-clear, bell-clear, was resonant with light. The river wormed its way under its gleaming, snail-trail skin, and Thomas was bent for Godstow along the bank, deliberating alone, true Thomas, walking so early.

It seemed to Thomas that Anna was unique – well, mad, really – in taking thought so seriously. Intuitively he was certain that the barrier between himself and her, which he had at first supposed to be her natural revulsion, her righteous anger at being manhandled so abruptly, was all in his own mind. His shame had proposed it to him; she had not. The more delicately he tried to deal with her the more dejected she became. The problem lay in the curriculum. Perhaps when one reached a sapless time of life, like Lightdown, it became possible to consider a work like *Cosi* coolly, and come to conclusions about it without making the smallest reference from it to questions in one's own life. But Anna was referring everything back directly, and refusing to start on a course which, it seemed, none could complete with honour.

And this did seem to Thomas mad. If he could talk her out of it, he thought, he must have a chance with her. After all, as the punk girl she had been vividly responsive . . . and on Mozart's logic, Thomas thought, the false self was the true one – hell, he was at it himself! It must be catching. It really was mad, wasn't it, to treat art like this, and propose to act or not to act accordingly? And yet, if thought was not for practical use, why was it so widely approved of? If nothing could be learned from art, why was art so important? He couldn't help seeing that a theorem demonstrated in music by Mozart possessed compelling force, and yet he was sure that no lesson from the past applied to him, now. So what if all those poor old sods had failed? He felt the world made new at daybreak that very morning, his own blood warm in the stinging cold. He knew his own feelings to be true, and stronger than any that had ever been felt in the whole world before him. How could one possibly compare what those boring, ugly, middle-aged folk had felt, ages ago, with what he was feeling? How could loving any ordinary sort of woman be like loving Anna? To love Anna as he did was self-validating!

But whereas dull, sublunary lovers' loves might wish for a tribute of flowers, might wish for gold and rubies, mad Anna, his wonderful crazy Anna, would be won with an argument. Just as well, perhaps, for arguments were within the reach of poor students, when rubies were not. He would, he resolved, excel himself. He would not try to argue for the irrelevance of art; instead he would resolve for Anna the whole conundrum of *Cosi*, he would demonstrate with incisive brilliance that it argued in favour of love; then things would matter again, she would be angry again, and together they would look for Lightdown's victims, save them, fall into each other's arms . . .

On the wide empty meadow Thomas ran round in circles, and jumped for joy. He mimed taking Anna in his arms, gently lifting her chin, and kissing her, for a stolid, mildly curious audience of bullocks; then he went racing home, full of eagerness to write.

At lunchtime Anna was surprised to see a chunky envelope sitting in her pigeonhole, which must have come by hand, since she took her morning letters earlier. She did not recognize the hand, and trotted up to her room with it full of curiosity. And found it was from Thomas. One handwritten sheet, and several typed ones. For a moment or two she was stricken – why write? why *write*? why not come? He must have come – as far as the pigeonholes in the front hall – and he had not come up. Perhaps he was in a tearing hurry; but she winced at the agony of having missed even a few moments with him, at perceiving that he saved himself the climb up a flight of stairs at the cost of not seeing her.

It took her some while to get round to reading the letter.

'Dearest Anna,' she read, 'This is to help you decipher the subtext I mentioned, which ought really to be called a supertext. I hope it helps. It isn't mine, of course, but is drawn from various great and good authorities. This is Taine, for example (sorry, my translation): "*On the stage there are two Italian flirts who laugh and lie; but in the music no-one lies, and no-one laughs; at the most one smiles; even tears are close to smiles . . .*" You see that I didn't make up the idea of a gulf between words and music, but I believe it. It explains everything, and relieves Mozart of the unjust charge of misogyny. Da Ponte can go to the devil where he belongs!'

Anna sat down on her rug, toasting her back at the fire, and spread out the typewritten sheets.

'Let me take you through it, stage by stage,' she read. 'As the opera opens we are confronted with four people, going through the motions of love, and full of false feeling. The two officers boast that each one's girl is super-special, rather as they might boast about their horses or swords. The girls gloatingly claim that each one's man is sublimely handsome . . . When the mock departure of the men is announced, the extravagant and disproportionate grief of the girls shows at once how full of vanity, how selfish and superficial their attachment to their partners really is. Who could honestly want to die because they are parting from a lover for a few months? The music leads our reactions – the early arias are cold and glittering, skits on *opera seria*, full of melodramatic effect. The parody is clear warning of the insincerity of the characters. The music of the cross-paired wooing likewise begins full of witty exaggeration and comic effect – the men are fooling, and the women are on high horses – the fun continues. The thing to notice, Anna dearest, is that only when the men woo with real feeling do the women waver and give in. Only in the new pairings do we begin to be able to tell the two men apart – Guglielmo witty, teasing and sensual, Ferrando tender and idealistic. The two girls are likewise different, a difference which only becomes apparent as we watch them responding to wooing – Dorabella light-hearted, hedonistic and amusing, Fiordiligi serious, self-respecting, and capable once awoken of fierce sexual passion. She does not give in until Ferrando, himself in grief, woos her sincerely, and implores her pity on pain which is perfectly genuine, though she does not know its source. Once again the music guides us in what to think. By the second act the music shows us lovers feeling the real thing for the first time. And the divergence between music and libretto is increasingly expressive. For example, as Fiordiligi struggles with temptation, the libretto gives her two lines, and Mozart lingers for eight bars of his most melting sympathy. It is impossible to believe that, knowing what they now know, the two couples return to their original grouping; the text gives us no clue, but the music has been eloquently lucid. They will marry their second choices. The opera does not attack love; it rejects insincere love in favour of true love. Similarly, the opera does not really attack women; the music has shown us vividly the infidelity perpetrated first by the men, who should not have been able, but have been able, to woo the wrong girls with feeling.

'As a matter of fact we know what both the authors of the opera thought about this. You remember the passage I copied from your notes, in which Da Ponte claimed that he had never aroused love he could not honourably satisfy – conduct which he clearly thought disgraceful, but which both the men in the opera have indulged in – while Mozart wrote to his father from Paris, "In my opinion there is nothing more shameful than to deceive an honest girl." In spite of the grammatical oddity of Italian, which can say "All women do it," or "Everybody does it," but not "All men do it," the opera does not so much attack women, as reject immature love, while celebrating the real thing.

'So there you have it. Nothing in it to bruise your hopes, dear Anna.

'Now, I'm sure you want some precise demonstration. Start by comparing Fiordiligi's first-act aria – "Like a rock . . ." with the second-act aria in which she asks for forgiveness for her weakness in being tempted; then listen carefully to the orchestration. A wonderfully beautiful combination of soft strings, wind, horn and human voice expresses fluently the real feeling, while whenever disguise and trickery are afoot, or false feeling is being expressed, Mozart replaces horns with trumpets, and a sharper, hard-edged sound emerges. Listen, and you'll agree.

'P.S. By the time you have listened, I shall have hired a car for the weekend. Meet you at 8.30 sharp at the college gate. Love, T.'

Was this a love letter? Not really. But it was a letter that implied love. Anna wanted to march round to Thomas's room right away and ask how he had found the money for the car, but instead she did what he wanted her to do. She sat down with the printed score and Thomas's letter in front of her, opened the box of tapes he had bought for her, and listened to the music.

Fleur thinks, 'Everything and everyone conspires against me. I must get out of here.' That's it! Why hadn't she thought of it before? The simple way to keep faith with William is to get the hell out of the house, remove herself – even, possibly, find a way to join William. Surely these days there is nowhere on the face of the earth to which one cannot get a package tour of some kind! It had been a terrible mistake to confide in Dora and Roz, but that would no longer matter if she got clean away. Deep inside her something starts to wail like an afflicted child at the thought of removing herself from Shiv; like an imperious parent she ignores it, and tells herself that she must go instantly, and leave no time for vacillation.

However, she cannot find her suitcase. When she had unpacked and settled in she had thrust it under the bed, and it is no longer there. She hastens downstairs again, calling for Roz.

'I put it in the boxroom,' Roz says.

'I want it back, please.'

Roz is kneading bread. 'Could it wait till I've got this in the oven, and washed the flour off my hands?' she says. 'I'll get it by suppertime.'

'Sorry, no. I'll get it myself if you tell me where to find the boxroom, but I must have it now.'

'I don't like the thought of you rummaging in the boxroom, thank you,' says Roz. 'I know where everything is at the moment. What's the hurry?

Anything you left in the case will be perfectly safe till supper.'

'I want it now,' says Fleur.

'All right, all right, hoity-toity,' says Roz, grimly, clapping her hands together to shake off the flour, and going to rinse them under the tap. 'I'll bring it to you.'

Fleur retreats to the tower bedroom, and waits. She looks at Dora's things lying beside the other bed, and wonders whether to go through the garden, and find Dora, and propose flight to her too. She could give Dora a lift . . . but of course she knows really that Dora would not come. Dora has given herself over to the charms of the young gardener, and the Lord knows what it would take to persuade her to miss going out with him tonight . . . Oh, does she herself really need to deny herself going out with Shiv? Yes, she does. The more she longs for it, the more clear it is that she mustn't do it.

Roz stumps into the room, and slams the suitcase down just inside the door. 'There you are, madam!' she says. 'In my opinion you're out of your tiny mind, but there it is. Now can I get back to my work?'

The moment she has gone Fleur begins to pack, flinging her clothes wildly into the case, and finding of course, that she cannot get the lid to close on them bundled and crumpled like that. Shaking, she tips the contents out, and starts again, folding them carefully. Then when the case is shut she goes and stands at the window. She imagines a scene on remote St Kilda, which in her mind's eye is a bit like Lundy Island, a few flat grassy acres standing up out of the sea on precipitous, friable cliffs. A ship has anchored off the landing, and she is stepping into a rowing boat to go ashore. Tall cliffs green with lichen and topped with a glory of gorse and heather tower above the black gravel of the sloping beach. A zigzag path of dizzy steepness ascends the cliff face, but she is dressed for climbing, in stout boots, and waxed rainproof trousers, and a windcheater. And at the top of the path she stands, scanning the entire island, a flat plateau, all within her view, and with a painful lurch of the heart she thinks for a minute that he isn't there; nobody is there. Has some terrible disaster encompassed them all? Then she sees a spike driven into the brink of the cliff on the further side of the island, and a clove hitch of red rope knotted round it. She runs, runs, looks over the edge – there far below, below the wheeling gulls, are William and his companions. When she calls he comes half leaping, half flying up to join her, and folds her in his arms. Not unnaturally, since he has obviously become weightless, his touch is ghostly and intangible. It does not assuage her longing.

'I must go to him,' says Fleur. She picks up her case, and starts down the stairs.

Thomas was cold. His breath clouded the interior of the cold car as he sat waiting for Anna in the bright mist of morning, at the door of her college. He was wearing a sweater, and a light raincoat, and his college scarf, but not the soft and windproof leather jacket, fleece lined, which his brother brought home for him from Morocco, and which had kept him warm this term so far, because he had sold that to pay for the car. Luckily that beast Martin had wanted it badly – there was money to spare in Thomas's pocket. Enough for a hot lunch, and even a hotel if their search took them far afield. The question was, would Anna come? Thomas thought she would, if she accepted his subtext. While he waited he studied the map, on which he had drawn a circle in red felt-tip, marking a fifty-mile radius of Oxford. If Lightdown was masterminding a nefarious plot in term time, Thomas thought, it would have to be reasonably nearby. Several volumes of Pevsner, borrowed from the library, were piled in the glovetray. Thomas could not think of an easier source of information on grand houses.

Although he was waiting for Anna he jumped when she suddenly opened the car door, and got in beside him. 'Oh! Anna . . .' he said.

She laughed. 'Weren't you expecting me? Are you waiting for somebody else?'

'No, of course not. I wasn't sure you would come. I thought you might not agree with me.'

'Can't I come unless I do? Because honestly, Thomas, I'm not sure that . . .'

'Of course you can. I just thought you wouldn't think it was worth it, unless I could de-disillusion you.'

'Thomas, I really don't need all that much persuasion to spend a day with you! And anything would be worth it to get our own back on the rattlesnake!'

'Well, I don't think it will be "anything", I think it will be quite fun. Bend your towering intellect to that map. I think Yarnton Manor first, and then Compton Wynyates. I'll steer, you navigate.'

'Ay, ay, Cap'n.'

Thomas looked joyfully down the street ahead, filled with golden mist, which the sun would soon drive away, shining with frost and topped with a clear blue sky. The day felt like treasure in his hands. He put the car in gear, and they were off.

It wasn't Yarnton. Yarnton had become a school, and no work was going forwards there. At Compton Wynyates they wandered hand in hand through the gardens, and stared at the rosy mellow perfection of the house, and then took a tour, and saw the secrets of the house, the sliding panels, the hidden rooms, the paintings and treasures. Thomas was entranced by the blue-gold-green tapestry of Cupid picking grapes. He longed to walk into the depicted vineyard and gather fruits of his own. 'Designed by a pupil of Raphael's', the guide informed them. Incredible, a fellow tour-taker said. But, Thomas thought, we are not an island in that sense. In art and literature and music England is stitched into the fabric of Europe, warp and weft. Didn't Mozart write symphonies in Chelsea? And what was Anna thinking, gazing at Cupid with her head slightly tilted, her expression reflective, her forehead smooth? He noticed that she liked the hangings, the bed curtains, the woven things, the Durham quilt. He had a vision of her, wearing dark velvet, sitting in the light of a high window, working with a needle, waiting. And realized that for all such Annas in the past the room was empty. Bygone Thomas was elsewhere, fighting, farming. Bygone Anna stitched because she had to do something, and it didn't matter what she thought. But present Anna's thoughts were all that mattered to him.

'Thomas, look, there's half a lifetime in this quilt,' she said.

'Wasted,' he said. 'Come, Anna, there's no-one here.'

By lunch-time they had visited five houses, asked in the lodges of three more, and found nowhere where work was going forward, and restorers or gardeners were living in. They were a little despondent, a little light-headed. Thomas was high on Anna's company; he had been with her longer continuously now by over an hour than ever before. The light they drove and parked and walked in was the varnished patina of winter noon, which apes the tonality of summer evenings. Anna had become a little, and Thomas very, cold. They stopped for a pub lunch.

There in the dark interior of the pub, lit mainly by a huge log fire that leapt and glinted on the horse brasses and the copper hunting horns, and the strange incunabula of rural things – hot-water jugs, trivets, goffering irons, bedpans – with which the blackened beams were hung, they ran to ground, settled comfortably on an ancient bench, which had skewed itself over years to conform to the undulations of the worn brick floor. From other tables a buzz of voices rose and fell like the light of the fire. Thomas and Anna ordered beer, flat and warm and as authentic as the panelling; and chose old English food, like breaded scampi and chilli with garlic bread, and ploughman's with Brie.

'Thomas, what's your essay subject this time?' Anna asked.

'Sisters. What's yours?'

'Life; Mozart's, that is.'

'Well, that sounds easy, anyway. Mine is deeply baffling.'

'It isn't easy at all! I can't make head or tail of it!' Anna protested.

'Sorry; I just thought there would be a lot known, and easily available and . . .'

'Well, there is. But it gives you such an uneasy feeling. People feel so strongly about him; he's covered all over with a sticky layer of adoration. It doesn't seem possible to discern him, somehow . . . everybody in turn is cutting him to fit a theory that doesn't seem quite right; like your theory of *Cosi*.'

'Wait; don't. Don't dismiss that out of hand. It's too important.'

'All right, tell me about sisters.'

'Well, I suppose that I'm supposed to be pursuing the possibility that the lives of Da Ponte and Mozart cast light on the opera. You must know all this. The first Fiordiligi was Adrienna Del Bene, and she was Da Ponte's mistress. The first Dorabella was her sister, Louise de Villeneuve. Da Ponte had been torn between two sisters once before. Don't I remember reading that he once went home through the streets, crying, "O Rosina! O Camiletta! O Camiletta! O Rosina! What will become of you?" convulsing his friend with laughter listening to that absurd lament. You know how you thought that the disguises which seem so absurd to us might have seemed OK to Da Ponte because of his life in Venice; well, perhaps the conduct of the men in so willingly and fervently wooing the wrong sister seemed OK to him because he regularly fancied any sister of a woman he loved . . . far from its being difficult to transfer your attentions to the other, he thought it was difficult to make up your mind.'

'And of course Mozart too had fallen in love with one sister, and then married another.'

'And was tended on his deathbed by a third.'

'Three is too many. It doesn't fit.'

'All right,' said Thomas, 'throw out Sophie. She doesn't fit.'

'But this might,' said Anna, rummaging in her bag. She brought out of her tattered bag a copy of Mozart's letters, full of dog-eared markers, and began to read to him:

'Dear Little Wife! I will be quite frank with you. You have no need to be unhappy. You have a husband who loves you and does all he can for you. As to your foot, you need only have patience. It will certainly get quite well. I am glad if you are in spirits – of course I am – only I

169

could wish you would not sometimes make yourself so cheap! You are too free, I think with blank, just as with blank when he was still in Baden. Consider that blank and blank are less free with other women, whom they know perhaps less well than they do you, than they are in your company! Even blank, who is otherwise a well-conducted man and particularly respectful towards women, must somehow have been misled into writing the most disgusting and coarsest sottises in his letter. A woman must always make herself respected or else she gets talked about. My dear! forgive me for being so frank, but my peace of mind demands it as well as our common happiness. Only remember that you once admitted to me yourself that you are inclined to be too compliant! You know the consequences of that. And remember, too, the promise you gave me. O God! Only try, my love – be merry and happy and kind with me – do not torment yourself and me with needless jealousy! have confidence in my love; you have proofs of it, surely! and you shall see how happy we will be. Do not doubt that it is only by her prudent behaviour that a woman can enchain her husband. Adieu; tomorrow I shall kiss you devotedly! Mozart.'

'Golly!' said Thomas. 'When did he write that?'

'August, 1789. He was writing *Cosi* in autumn and winter of that year. He was writing *Cosi* while Constanze was in Baden, recuperating.'

'What was wrong with her?'

'Something to do with her foot. She outlived him by fifty years.'

'What are all those blanks doing?'

'She and her second husband did a lot of

170

scratching things out, obliterating names and such-like after his death. Many of his letters are partly defaced.'

'So he definitely got the wrong sister.'

'The one he would have preferred said later that she knew nothing of his genius, she just thought of him as a little man.'

'Oh.'

'And, Thomas, there's no point at all in thinking that he ought not to have loved Constanze; he just did. Here – take the book, and read his letters to her – any letter to her!'

They were silent, thinking sorrowfully. Above Thomas's head a complex of dancing glints of firelight clustered on the beam. Anna could not decipher it. But here came their food, laid on the brown board in front of them, and very welcome.

'So to sum up,' said Thomas, as they sipped their coffee, 'there were two men in deep difficulty, working on this opera. Both had reason to think all women did it. Da Ponte was in a three-sided relationship with a married woman, and on perfectly friendly terms with her husband; Mozart's wife was causing scandal, flirting openly with other men in Baden.'

'You mean, it wouldn't be surprising if they concocted a bitter and cynical opera?'

'But they didn't. You know what I think about that.'

'Yes. I don't agree with you. But isn't it all odd? So circumstantial and curious. As if when you looked closely at the facts there was never a pattern, and yet, out of the corner of your eye . . .'

'You also can't help thinking if you stared longer, there would be a pattern after all.'

'What next?' said Anna, putting down her empty cup, and picking up her bag.

'Odder and odder,' said Thomas. 'Within a couple of years of that opera Da Ponte has broken with Del Bene; he plays the most monstrous trick, trying to get himself out of trouble by shopping her husband to the authorities, giving them papers he must have got hold of through her. And then he took up with another woman to whom he was faithful all the rest of his life, and set out on adventures that all turned out respectable. While Mozart . . .'

'Struggled in vain to get out of debt, fell ill and died. Herr Sussmayer, who was certainly one of those men that Constanze was indiscreet with, did a bunk, and Constanze embarked on a career as a widow, and defacer of letters.'

They stood up to go. Thomas stood between the dancing fire and the brasses on the ceiling beam.

'Oh, look,' said Anna. 'I couldn't make out what this was in the firelight; in the shadow you see at once, it's the sun-in-splendour.'

'Do they all have names?' asked Thomas, as they walked into the raw cold of the car park.

'Only some. I happen to know that one.'

'And Anna? Do you have any sisters?'

Anna laughed. 'Sorry, you're out of luck. There's only me.'

'Thank heaven for that!' said Thomas. 'Find Stanton Harcourt on the map, Anna. There next.'

In the main hall Fleur stops. She puts down the case in the middle of the floor, and turns aside to the music room. The faint smell of solvent that lingers there ravishes her memory with images of Shiv lying supine, the glass broken in his outflung hand . . . and only a split second behind comes memory of his naked body, being laid in white sheets, tactile and

172

visual recall of the warmth and glory of his dark and golden skin. She closes the door of the music-room behind her, and, seeing a key in the lock, locks it. And now in safety she can contemplate her unfinished task.

Two of the panels in the room are bright and clear. She must originally have underestimated them; they are full of a warm radiance, and a flowing, witty line. The artist was a good draughtsman, as well as a good colourist, and he delineated somehow as if he thought it was amusing, unlikely even, that anything should be so summery and fair. The third panel she has not yet touched. She flips on the lights, and stares at it. It shows a feast of some kind, public rejoicing. A boy in the foreground plays a lute, and another, a black boy, is lifting a silver trumpet to his pursed lips. Beyond, a table is laid with blurred and indecipherable mounds of fruit and game. There are two couples seated at the table, and in each couple the girl appears to be writing on a parchment. Signing something? The parchment is smoothed out in front of the girl on the left by the dark stranger from the other pictures. The girl on the right is taking hers from the hands of a smiling young woman. Beside each girl a man is sitting, leaning tenderly towards her, encircling her shoulders with an embracing arm . . . Suddenly Fleur is deeply afraid.

The picture strikes her with terror as vivid and as pure as if it were a dance of death. From the clothes of both men and women she can see that the *dramatis personae* are the same as in the other two panels. If she cleaned the faces she would know which girl was sitting with which man . . . But whatever her contract says, whatever the owner may think of her, she knows that she does not want to clean the third picture, and that the message contained in it is something she doesn't want to know.

173

And then she hears behind her the light percuss-
ive notes of the tumblers turning in the lock; she is
not safe, after all. Someone is pursuing her, using
another key.

'Who let you in?' she says. 'Get out of here!'

'You are leaving?' It is his voice – she has not
looked round – but loaded with pain. 'You intend to
go, and let me die of misery?'

Still she stands, facing the picture, not turning her
head. He strides across the room, and stands facing
her across the work table, still covered with her
paraphernalia. With the side of his dark hand he
sweeps a clearance, and taking a silver-hilted,
jewelled dagger from inside his jacket he lays it, hilt
towards her in front of her. She barely glances at it –
a barbarous thing – because she is staring at his face.
That mockery, that submerged laughter that she
once saw there has gone. The expression he fixes on
her is one of agony. He has been weeping, surely; his
eyes are reddened and the pupils are distended. The
corners of his tender and sensuous mouth are pulled
taut with pain. He cannot be dissembling . . .

'You might as well take this,' he says to her,
drawing the knife from its theatrically decorated
sheath, and handing it to her, 'and stab me through
the heart. That would at least be quick, be merciful!'

'Oh, stop it . . .' she says.

'Do you hesitate?' he asks. 'I'll show you. Thumb
on the blade, and strike upwards – let me guide your
hand!'

'Don't, don't,' she says, backing away from him.
'Haven't I been tormented enough, made unhappy
enough?' But it is his unhappiness, not hers, that
speaks between them.

His wild manner is suddenly stilled. He puts
down the ridiculous knife. 'What do you mean?' he
says. 'Have I tormented you? What can you mean?

You must mean you have begun to love me . . .'

'Oh, what am I to do?' she cries. 'How can I contend with this?'

'Dearest, pity me!' he says, very softly. 'Without you, life is death to me. Take pity on me, and I will be all in all to you, I will be husband and lover, I will be mother and father to you, bedmate and body-slave . . .'

'Ah, you are ruthless!' she says. 'You are cruel! But you win – I can't go on fighting you. ' Her desire for him engulfs her, like the tide overwhelming a sand dam on the shore. 'Do whatever you will with me . . .'

'This first, then,' he says, and seizing her he kisses her fiercely. He is holding her hard against him, and she feels the thrusting tension of his body, the thrusting hunger of his mouth and tongue. Every nerve of her own body answers and consents. She surprises him. When at last he stands back from her he is looking at her with a sort of ravenous astonishment. He looks wildly round the room, which contains no sort of soft horizontal surface. 'I'll book a room for us tonight,' he says. 'And then, oh God, love . . .'

He has gone. Her knees seem to have turned to water. She thinks of him undressing for her, she thinks of his body taut on top of hers like a drawn bow. Shaking, she sits down abruptly in the nearest dustsheeted little chair, and finds herself in front of the first panel, bright and clean as if painted that morning, from which the diabolical dark stranger laughs at her with vicious glee.

The car chugged steadily through little lanes, as they planned a route swinging round Oxford clockwise, looking for houses, magnificent or obscure. From

Brill and Islip, Hinksey and Eynsham, to Stanton Harcourt by and by. There was a tower in a cowy field, in which, the book says, Pope wrote the *Essay on Man*. Nothing was happening in it now. And then they found themselves in a village. A perfect village, such as one still, though increasingly seldom, happens on in England. It was made of a tight little street of stone houses, some with doll's-house grandeur, most snug and small. The line of houses, punctuated by stretches of garden wall, ran up a slope to hug the lower margins of a wood spreading over the hilltop. The church had almost buried itself in the wood, but its tower stood clear. Stone monuments crowded shoulder to shoulder in the churchyard as though flocking up from street to porch. In the low brightness of the afternoon, the wonderful perpendicular lights of a fine clerestory were lit from both sides, so that the church glowed like burnished pewter. At the bottom of the street a tiny bridge spanned the watersplash through the stream that any car must take, to the vocal annoyance of a mongrel assortment of white and brown ducks.

And the street was muddy; two real and active farmyards opened into it, their barns the largest and the grandest things below the church, and a slowly swaying and bellowing chorus of black and white cows was crossing by the traffic lights, bringing Thomas to halt the car. They watched the mild brutes passing, and a cluster of white doves flying in and out of a barrel-shaped cote in the farmyard.

'Let's look at that church,' said Thomas.

They parked at the lych gate, and climbed the path. When they reached the door the muted drone of music was leaking faintly to them through oak and stone and glass. A service? Not on a weekday. They went in. A stout and floridly complexioned elderly man, wearing tweeds that could have doubled as sandpaper, was playing. They walked quietly, looking. Everything was neat and dry, the candlesticks shining, the flowers fresh. An exotically unusual font sprouted stiff flowers in full relief. It was undoubtedly powerfully ancient. An arch in the tower was carved with dogtooth, and there was a wonderful boss in the tower roof, above the bell-ropes, – a wildly foliate green man.

The organist was rather good. But he finished as they finished looking round, and folded his music ...

'How beautifully kept this church is,' said Anna politely.

'We do try,' he said. 'We try to keep things as they ought to be. Just passing, are you?'

'We are looking for someone, as a matter of fact,' said Thomas. 'A friend of ours is working somewhere around here doing restoration work on the furnishings of an old house. We lost the address. We are looking for a house with something in progress ...'

'Ah,' said the organist. 'Well, not mine, I'm afraid. Mine has all the grooming it's going to get before I die. In trust for my nephew, the whole thing ... but there's a neighbour of mine ... I wonder ... ?'

And suddenly their luck changed. The lord of the manor disapproved of his neighbour – never there, that fellow – who had let his house and garden go to rack and ruin, and then quite suddenly employed some young people to work on it. Without asking the V and A. Mind you, Roseguard always was a pickle of a house ... Yes indeed, he would direct them.

'Thank you,' said Anna as they left. 'And for the music.'

'Lovely thing, isn't it?' the lord of the manor said. 'We've a wedding tomorrow, and people always ask for that. No health service then, of course.'

'Luckily for us,' said Anna smiling.

'What was that about?' said Thomas, opening the car for her.

'He was paying the Ave Verum.'

'That I realized . . .'

'Mozart tossed it off to repay a *kapellmeister* who was looking after Constanze in Baden . . . Thomas, we must go quickly now. It's getting dark.'

'The bitch!' cries William. 'The filthy, stinking bitch!'

'What? You mean even unarranged girls may not have meant what they said?' says Ferdy, bitterly.

'I'm sorry, Ferdy,' says William. 'I deserved that. But, God! what do they deserve, and how shall we get our own back?'

'First confront them, then marry them!' says Alfie, triumphant. 'You will forgive them, with delectable superiority and magnanimity; how enjoyable that will be! Then, my dears, you will allow me to take you dancing next week, as I wanted to do in the first place, and you will feel not a twinge of guilt – don't you see how I have liberated you? Marriage without chains will in due course be yours.'

'Alfie, you don't understand what you have done,' says William. 'We can't marry them now.'

'Ah, well,' says Alfie, shrugging. 'A bachelor's life has many advantages. Many varied pleasures and few real deprivations.'

'But not for me,' says William. 'I have never had the least difficulty getting girls. There's many fine fish in the sea.'

'Certainly,' says Ferdy. 'We can pick and choose as we please. We shan't lack for women.'

'Of course not; but if these two, – these wonderful,

special, noble souls, so faithful, so high-minded, so well-bred . . .'

'Oh, belt up, Alfie!' cries Ferdy.

'. . . could do this to you, how will the rest behave? It's a law of nature and there are no exceptions. If they change their heart's affiliation a thousand times a day don't blame them, accept it — they're only human. And it isn't a vice, you know, in a poor silly creature, to feed the heart's hunger; as she sees it, — and I agree with her — it's a necessity. And after all, you still love them, don't you? these plucked birds of yours!'

Ferdy meets William's eyes. How has it happened that something which so short a time ago was pure joy — 'I love her, I love her!' they had told each other, laughing — had become now so bitterly painful?

'I wish I didn't,' says William, miserably, 'but, oh! I do.'

And that is the minute Roz chooses to put her head round the door of Alfie's room, and to say brightly, 'Good luck to all smart operators! I've made perfectly sure that they know you have booked bedrooms as well as tables. I've nudged and winked, and told them the reception clerk is a friend of mine and has told me all about it, and neither one nor the other is backing out! They are bathing and dressing and putting on lipstick right now! Aren't you pleased?'

'Delighted,' says Ferdy, through clenched teeth.

'What I don't understand,' said Thomas, 'is why you don't agree with me. You haven't explained. And I was so sure the music would convince you!'

They were driving in a winding road between hedgerows, while the sun slipped down far enough

179

to blaze on the serpentine scrawl of a little stream threading between willows in the fields on their right.

'The trouble with your theory is that it makes sense . . .'

'What are theories for?'

'But the opera doesn't. Not neat, reasonable sense like that. It's prickly; it refuses to fit.'

'You are cavalier with your accusations.'

'I'm not accusing; I'm excusing, rather. But it's the essence of *Cosi* not to fit. It doesn't leave you full of glowing contentment, like *Figaro*; it doesn't leave you feeling that the wicked will be judged, and justice will prevail, like *Don Giovanni*. It leaves you uneasy, puzzled, stung in some way. Not just me; everybody. If your theory were correct it wouldn't do that.'

'But it's so clear. You follow the pretence right through, like the trumpets. The original pairings are phoney, and they remain so, so that when the men "return" from the war that note is still sounding . . . oops!'

For he had driven them through a water splash, rather faster than was prudent. 'Now try your brakes,' said Anna. 'And suppose you were right, that would certainly empty the opera of relevance, Thomas. Talk about an inapplicable lesson!'

'What do you mean?'

'Well, you say it is intent upon making a distinction between false and true love. But at any particular time, how would one know whether the love one was feeling was the phoney, exaggerated kind, or the real thing? Once we are in love, are we placed as the lovers are at the opening of the opera or as they are later with the second wooers? How do we know? It's all very well to say "*finem lauda*" but one lives life forwards. Do you think the characters

180

in Act One of the opera know their feelings are false?'

'Then, according to you, what does the element of parody mean?'

'I don't think the element of parody makes it clearly mean thus and thus. I think it makes it unclear what it means. It just shimmers with ambivalence . . . Then, again, Thomas, on your theory it would be gross, an offence against self-knowledge, against true love, against everyone's chance of happiness, if at the end they simply hopped into bed with their original partners. And I know the text doesn't actually say they do; I know it can be produced with them marrying the new lovers. But somehow that feels tricksy to me; flying in the face of the probabilities.'

'What probabilities do you mean?'

'Well, think how triumphant Don Alfonso is. Henceforward they will be wiser, and do what he tells them. But if they were in the arms of new sweethearts, they would surely be taking love seriously again, and would need teaching again — don't you see?'

'Hmm. Was Diomede, do you think, perfectly confident of Cressida's loyalty? But it does occur to me that those girls didn't really fall in love with each other's fellow. They fell in love with a pair of un-inhibited and preposterous Albanians, who simply didn't exist.'

'Like the punk girl,' thought Anna, wincing, 'whom poor Thomas loves.'

'The hell with them!' said Thomas suddenly. 'Anna, it isn't what they did we should be talking about, but about what we . . .'

'Oh, look!' she cried, 'That sign said "Roseguard". Back up, Thomas. We've overshot the turn.'

*　　　*　　　*

Roz is sitting on the corner of the bed, watching
Dora brush and plait her shining midnight hair. She
is braiding it with silk ribbons threaded with
sequins. She is wrapping herself in diaphanous gold
chiffon, setting a jewel in the corner of her nose, and
a luscious caste mark on her forehead. Fleur in her
simple dress of blue silk, her pearls, her touch of
powder feels upstaged, and watches enviously. A
little electric fire brought up from somewhere
downstairs glows in the corner of the room, but the
sense of warmth, of close intimacy, of shared
excitement is really the current flowing between the
room's occupants, needing no artificial fire to start
its smouldering.

Turning from the mirror to gaze at Fleur, Dora
says, 'Borrow these! they'll look lovely with that
dress – just right – see?' and she gathers up from her
jewel box a handful of fine glass bangles in deep
midnight blue, and threads them on to Fleur's wrist.

'Don't you want them yourself?' Fleur asks,
tempted.

'I'm wearing this,' – Dora points to a pretty little
gold pendant on a chain round her neck – 'and
enough is enough.'

'What about the flowers?' Roz asks. 'Aren't you
going to wear them?'

'Flowers?' asks Dora.

'Oh, how silly of me! I brought them up to you,
and then forgot to mention them. They're here.'

There on the table are two florist's boxes in clear
Perspex, each containing an orchid, prepared to
wear. Nestling in the mist of fern round each
blossom is a tiny card, and both cards say, 'To the
loveliest girl in England.'

182

'Which is which?' says Fleur, taking the white flower and trying it against her dress, looking in the mirror.

'How awfully gallant of them!' says Dora, laughing. 'I didn't know Englishmen still did this sort of thing.' The deep red bloom flecked with gold is looking wonderful on the shoulder of her sari. 'Or perhaps . . .' she says, edging into the mirror beside Fleur; and twisting up her plait into a shell-like tapering curl on her head, she tries the flower in her hair.

'Bother!' says Fleur, picking up the card from Dora's flower. 'Look at the initials on the message. I've got yours, and you've got mine.'

They exchange flowers and try again. The dark red flower shows sombrely out of key on Fleur's blue silk. The white flower shows brightly against Dora's dark hair, but until she put it there every highlight on Dora had been gold, gold picking up the glow on her honey-coloured skin. White is the last thing, really . . .

'Would it be awful to wear the wrong one?' asks Dora.

'They might be hurt.'

'Use your wits!' suggests Roz. 'If they notice, just say the florist must have muddled the order!'

'Of course,' says Dora, dropping the flower back into the wrong box, and handing it to Fleur.

So the two of them, smiling, exchange flowers again, and help each other, Fleur gently easing the foil-wrapped stem of the red flower into the heavy rope of Dora's hair, until nothing but the flower shows; Dora carefully placing and pinning the white one on Fleur's dress.

'You look perfectly lovely!' Fleur says.

'And you too! Really!'

Smiling, and arm in arm, they descend, and then

stand waiting discreetly out of sight of the entrance hall, in the gallery that goes towards the music room. Soon there is a crunch of a car on gravel, a knock on the door. Roz appears, visibly gleeful, and says, 'There's a young man here for Dora.'

Fleur kisses Dora. 'Have a wonderful time,' she whispers.

'You too, you too – let yourself go!' says Dora, departing.

Fleur paces softly in the dim light of the room. She allows herself to think about what Roz told her earlier – that Shiv, good as his word, has booked a room in the hotel where he is taking her to dinner. She smiles to think that if she had been asked, instead of just told, she might have felt obliged to object. But now she feels her own flesh warm upon her bones. She is suffused with the expectation of joy.

Another knock on the door; then he is standing in the rotunda, under the glittering brilliance of the chandelier. She moves slowly out of the shadows to join him. 'Do you know,' he says to her, 'until the last minute – until this very moment – I was not sure that you would come?'

'Oh. Why?' she says, as he takes her coat from her arm, and holds it for her to slip into.

'That other fellow of whom you talk so much . . .' he says.

'You have struck me with total oblivion,' she says. 'I have no past now, only prospects.'

'Come, then,' he says, putting an arm round her shoulders, and leading her out.

'So that's that,' says Roz to the empty hall, as the door closes behind them. 'I've done my bit. Very successfully, too. It isn't everybody who could have managed it, but I'm pretty sharp really, pretty cool. And I think I'll slip off and find him at once, and collect what he promised me before he changes his mind. You can't trust an old bastard like that one.'

The narrow lane was bright with the golden misty globes of the seed heads of traveller's joy, collecting the setting sun. Skeletal flower heads brown and stiff with age brushed the sides of the car, and the hawthorn hedge flaunted its useless bright berries in profusion. It was a surprisingly busy road for such a by-way; Thomas had to pull in to very tight passing places three times for oncoming cars.

Then suddenly a sharp bend in the road left them facing a gateway, with wrought iron gates standing wide, and a grassy overgrown drive ahead. Thomas stamped on the brakes, dazzled by the sunset streaming through the gates, and then drove on. And there ahead of them, made all of lilac shadow against the light, was a beautiful classical house, and the looming bulk of what seemed like part of a castle behind it. The pale stone of its details, columns, steps, architraves, answered the evening in pink and gold. They wandered first through the gardens, finding the walks and dark bowers in the obscure dusk. A rose garden greeted them with dimly visible blooms in shadowy foliage, and a perfume so intense and faint it ravished and faded within the instant. Soon they found a barrow-load of topiary clippings, a straight line marking an edge over-powered by creeping thyme, signs of work. The doors of the house were unlocked, the house empty and unlit. Going in they called, timidly, softly, and got no answer. So they wandered, putting on and switching off lights, finding the rooms dust-sheeted, the paintings coggled in their frames, the ormolu cracked, the cushions and tapestries frayed

. . . They climbed to another floor and kept looking.

'Are we sure there has to be work going forward in the house as well as the garden?' Anna asked. 'Where did we get that idea from?'

'I don't remember,' Thomas said. They climbed another stair, and suddenly saw light above them. 'Hold on. There's somebody here we can ask.'

'Thomas, don't!' said Anna, hanging back. 'We're trespassing, aren't we?'

But Thomas had leapt ahead of her, up a narrow turning stair, and rather than be left behind in the dark, she went after him.

He went up and up. And then knocked on a door, and opened it to a faint, 'Come in,' behind it.

They found themselves standing in the door of a bedroom, or rather of a sitting room containing a bed, on which a man was lying. He turned his head, and they could see at once that he could not turn his body. A fire was burning in the grate. A book was propped in a gadget that held it for him, beside the bed.

'Company!' he said. 'Wonderful!'

'Can you help us?' said Thomas. 'We are looking for a house with some work going forward – with two young women, doing the sort of work for which one might live in for a few weeks, and we wondered if it could be here . . .'

'What are the names of these two?' the man asked.

'We don't know.'

'What kind of work are they doing, exactly?'

'I'm afraid we don't know that either. Perhaps restoring things?'

'You don't seem to know much about them,' the man said.

'We think, you see,' said Anna, 'that someone is playing a trick on them. If we could find them we could warn them.'

'But you know that warnings are always too late. And besides, I don't believe you.'

'But . . .' Thomas sounded indignant.

'I would say that you two had found what you were looking for,' the invalid said. 'I congratulate you on the ingenuity of your excuse for running around together, but it is extravagantly absurd.'

'We only want to know if you know . . .' Thomas resumed. Privately he concluded that they were talking to a madman.

'I'll tell you what you want to know,' the man interrupted him. 'I have a lot of time for thinking. And I find that I have repented, sometimes bitterly, of things that I did not do; regretted them painfully. But I have never felt a moment's trepidation, or a morsel of guilt over anything that I did do, whether it turned out well or ill. Does that help?'

'Yes,' said Anna, amazing Thomas. 'Yes, it does. Thank you.'

'Dear girl,' the man said, trying to keep looking at her, but failing to keep his head turned for long, so that it rolled back, diverting his gaze. 'Do you have any influence over the beautiful young man standing beside you? Will you ask him to kiss me?'

Anna's eyes, wide with amazement, met Thomas's. Silently she asked him. Thomas coloured up, but he went forward at once, and bent over the invalid, and kissed him. And he was, once he was doing it, she saw, magnanimous, taking the locked, clenched hand in his own hand, smoothing the tousled hair on the man's forehead, and kissing him twice.

'Your heart's desire to both of you, but do get on with it!' said the man, sighing, as Thomas straightened. 'Remember, this isn't a rehearsal. There are no retakes, no further performances. Life plays live, so to speak; and it's curtains in no time.'

'Where could we go to be safe and comfortable?'

Thomas asked, admitting the true quest, admitting the stranger as an ally. His question did not send Anna in full flight down the stairs.

'There are plenty of bedrooms here,' the man said. 'But not much cheer, I admit. Try the Rose Revived, down by the river. That used to be cosy.'

'Anna,' said Thomas, as they got back into the car, 'Anna, I've been wanting to say to you . . . to explain . . .' They sat together, shivering, while their breath on the cold windscreen misted over, and blotted out the dawning stars. 'I've been so sorry,' he said. 'It was so awful of me to grab you like that. I've never done anything like that before, and it's not how I feel about you; I love you truly, Anna, and tenderly, and I thought if I treated you very gently, very respectfully, you would see that I honour you, I adore you, and you would let me take it back . . .'

'I saw you were taking it back,' she said. 'It's been breaking my heart.'

'But . . . didn't you mind it?'

'Did it seem at the time as though I minded? It was the most wonderful thing that ever happened to me. If it happened to me, that is. I thought perhaps it happened to the punk girl.'

'Oh, Anna!' exclaimed Thomas, 'I assumed . . . I mean all this time I thought . . . I mean, that isn't how one is supposed to treat a girl!'

'I'm not a girl,' she said. 'I am Anna. You treat me as Anna. Who loves you.'

'Oh, my darling,' said Thomas, 'do you mean that if I can find us a room at some pub or somewhere, you will let me start again, you will let me try again, and this time take the whole thing slowly?'

'*No*, Thomas,' she said, emphatically, so that for a whole second of agony he thought he had misunderstood, that all was after all lost . . .

'Not slowly!' she said.

You see the lights of the Rose Revived, the string of coloured bulbs along the roofline, the brightly lit pub sign swinging on the roadside post, the golden windows, a little way before the narrow bridge. The rise of the bridge arch gives you a moment's dazzling glimpse of all the lamplight and window light shining double, hanging in banners slashed to ribbons in the silken water; then you turn into the car park, in thick darkness, made total by the contrast with the bright lights over the door into the building. As you get out of your car the sound of the river flows into the surrounding night. There is a path round to the terrace, to a riverside garden, and to the floodlit bridge, inviting couples to wander and dally under the stars. A bird – could it be a nightingale? – perhaps only a thrush staying up later than usual – sings wildly somewhere in the sallows by the bank beyond the bridge. And the night is as cool as the dark river; a night sharply cold for summer, balmy for autumn.

Getting out of the car, her silk dress whispering to her movements, Fleur looks round her avidly. One does not usually know, one does not foresee, which moments, which places will be those that inhere for ever in the memory, and make the bedrock of one's vision of the world. That this place will be such, she does know. 'This is Illyria, lady,' she tells herself. Shiv is handing her out of the car. Beyond the line of the building she sees in the light playing on the bridge the shadowy outline of two figures, young people, leaning close to each other, leaning on the bridge, looking down at the sounding water. Shiv takes her arm, and they go in.

The room is warm, with a fire leaping in an antique hearth. They find a quiet table, screened between facing oak pews, and sit down. She faces him across the table. Looking at him makes her dizzy. He does not quite meet her glance, or only for split seconds. That curious sense of play, of delicate amusement, with which he courted her so extravagantly, has modulated now into something else. He is standing himself off from her direct, exploring gaze, holding himself in waiting.

The room is filling up. People are moving on the edge of her field of vision. Someone has come to sit down on the opposite side of the inglenook, hidden behind a copy of *The Times*. A streak of black, a streak of gold – a couple are crossing the ends of the pew, entering the corner of her vision as they walk together . . . the reader lowers the copy of *The Times*, and grins – Mr Lightdown? Then Dora's voice, raised, acid, 'Ferdy, what in the name of hell do you think you're doing here, with another woman? – oh, God! – with Fleur?'

And Fleur looks round and sees Dora standing there, with William.

William says, uncertainly, 'Fleur, what are you doing . . . ?'

'I thought you were on St Kilda, William!' she says, appalled.

'William?' says Dora. 'This is Jim. This is my gardener – aren't you, Jim?'

'Well, I, er . . . I can explain,' says William.

'And who,' says Fleur, very softly, staring at Shiv, 'are you?'

'It's a joke!' says William brightly. 'A bet. I'm afraid you've lost it for us. He can explain – he got us into this!' And he points at Mr Lightdown, staring grimly at them from behind his lowered *Times*.

'Rubbish!' snaps Dora. '*He* hasn't been courting either of us. Fleur, when you talked to me about the assistant restorer, the man you meant was this fellow here, I am to understand? You have been talking about my Ferdy?'

Fleur nods, biting her lips.

'And everything I have told you about the gardener was the doing of this wretch, who all the time was supposed to be committed to you!'

'It was only in fun!' says William. 'And it was fun, wasn't it? It was only a bet.'

'You were making fools and whores of us for money!' says Dora, splendidly angry. 'Ferdy; you didn't need money. How *could* you?'

'How could *you*, Dora?' he says sullenly. 'That's the real point. How hurtful it is to know that some bloody Englishman can have you for the asking!'

'Come, Fleur,' says Dora, quietly. 'It is time we were going. Come with me.'

But Fleur, white and rigid, is still looking across the table at Ferdy. 'Tell me,' she says, 'everything you said to me; everything you said you felt for me; was there any truth at all in any of it? Didn't you mean even half a syllable of it?' For she thought she had known when he changed tone with her, when it was no longer a game between them. Now, for example, his face is full of pain. His eyes flinch away from hers; he looks at Dora, and says, 'There was not a syllable of truth in one word of it.'

'You simply didn't mean it?' She needs to make him repeat it.

'I honestly didn't mean it . . .' He is still looking at Dora. So that, although she knows he is lying, she knows also, since he denies himself, there is no hope for her. She gets up, and walking past Dora's extended hand, she strides, and then runs, for the door. Dora turns on her heel and follows her.

'We were going to have a wonderfully enjoyable time forgiving them, were we?' says Ferdy, bitterly.

'Women don't know their place, these days,' says

191

Alfie in an almost equally mordant tone. 'The modern hussy is not as easily shamed as the eighteenth-century one. Sorry, dear boys. Believe me, all's well that ends badly. Let me buy you a stiff drink. And wait till you see the lovelies I have lined up for you next week.'

'You pig, Alfie!' cries Ferdy, 'You absolute turd! You really don't know what kind of a beast you've let out of the bag, and can't get back in again, do you? William, I don't know what you think of doing, but I'm going to try to retrieve matters. They can't have gone far; we've got the car keys.'

And William follows him out.

The inn looked charming when they found it – a fine old stone building in a garden on the riverbank, where the Thames ran softly, to an eternally deferred song's end. They caught a glint of light, a streak of silver, where some nocturnal creature ferried across the water. The car park was rather full, and grandly togged people seemed to be dashing across it hither and yon. Thomas couldn't find a space. He turned with difficulty.

'Those people can't have an idea how hard they are to see in the dark, tearing about like that!' he grumbled. He drove out of the car park, and across the bridge, turned, and returned, and found a field gate where he could pull off the road. They were facing the inn now across the shining river, under the bare branches of a winter tree, in which the stars seemed tangled like fireflies in a web. The moment he stopped the car he put an arm round Anna, and buried his head in her shoulder. She took his hand.

'Content?' she asked.

'Beyond anything. I'll go and see if they have a

room. They look rather busy. We might be out of luck.'

'Go and try. I'll wait.'

'Will you be all right?'

'Perfectly. And you?'

'Oh, perfectly,' Thomas said. 'I think I am about to have everything the heart desires.'

'And then nothing left to wish for? That sounds rather alarming. Surely not, Thomas.'

'Well, only . . .'

'Something, then. What?'

'It would have been good if we had worked it out so as to have Mozart's blessing. He seemed so important all the while we were falling in love; I wish we didn't just have to ignore him now!'

'Go and see about the room,' she said, smiling at him in the dark.

'Dora!' calls Ferdy, stumbling about in the dark. He narrowly avoids walking into the path of a car. He cannot find her in the car park. He goes round into the garden on the riverbank, full of shadowy bushes and trees, and gropes his way along the terrace, still yelling for her. At the far end of the garden where it peters out alongside the river, and sheds itself into the water in a flurry of irises and arrowhead, serenely gleaming in the faint light of a rising half-moon, there is a garden bench, and there she sits. He does not see her in the darkness until she moves, in a burst of faintly golden highlights on her sari. She does not answer him. He sits down on the other end of the bench.

'It will be very embarrassing if we break off our engagement,' he says. 'Think how the aunties will gossip and laugh!'

'That is entirely up to you, Ferdy,' she says. 'You seem to think yourself aggrieved.'

'Well, but I am, I am!' he says. 'You gave away my portrait!'

'I was going to get it back. I was going out to dinner, and then I was going home.'

'Do you expect me to believe you? He had booked a room.'

'But so had you.'

'It's different for a man, as you very well know.'

'But so unkind, Ferdy. Very hurtful to me, and abominably cruel to her.'

'There was nothing in it. Just a game.'

'As I say, abominably cruel. She was really falling for you, you know!'

'Was she?' At that thought a flash of yearning, a moment's grieving of horrible intensity burns him. He is glad it is too dark for Dora's beady eyes to scan his face.

'What are you going to do?' she asks.

'Oh, I am going to forgive you, and things will be as they were,' he says.

'Then I shall make you a faithful wife, Fernando,' she says.

'I believe you, my darling, but . . .'

'But?'

'But perhaps I will be treating you a little more than I might have done like a traditional husband. Perhaps you will have a woman friend with you when you go out, perhaps your demeanour will be Eastern.'

'Certainly, Ferdy. And now that I know what you can get up to in three days, you will get a traditional insanely jealous and watchful wife!'

He laughs. He feels in a way enormous relief; for this picture of husband and wife is both comic and familiar. He is rediscovering what he always knew.

'Ferdy?' she says. Her voice is soft and vibrant. 'Marry me soon.'

It takes William some time to find Fleur. When he does, what he finds is the sound of someone weeping. The sound seems to come from the depths of a bosky wood, a shrubby part of the riverbank on the other side of the road from the pub. He calls to her. At first his calling makes no difference, then it produces silence. A bird sings into the rest on the soprano stave.

'Fleur?' he asks the silence. 'Do come out of there, and let's talk.'

'Go away,' comes an answer at last.

'Darling Fleur, do listen. I forgive you; I forgive you with all my heart!'

'Fuck off!' she replies.

He leans against a tree trunk, and considers. 'This is an awful mess,' he tries. 'Believe me, darling, I had misgivings about it. But I didn't realize how much you might be hurt. And I see now how stupid that was, but please, Fleur, forgive me. Forgive me, and come out of there, and let's talk.'

When he gets no reply he begins to fight his way through the branches in the rough direction of the voice. The bird above them flies off in fright, and the bushes rustle and crack at his every movement.

'William! Leave me alone,' says Fleur. 'You can't do anything for me. You are the last person – do you hear? – the last person that I ever want to see – you are abominable, beneath contempt, you are . . .' She breaks off as a loud splash announces William's fall into the river. Neither of them had realized that a tributary branch was flowing between them.

She does feel a tiny stab of remorse. After all, it is not really the enormity of William's conduct, dreadful though that is, that is making her pour forth her heart abroad in ecstasies of grief. Then desolation overcomes her again, and she resumes her racking weeping.

Luckily William is a good swimmer. Gasping with cold and surprise he is swept downstream through the arches of the bridge below the confluence, and scrambles ashore in the pub garden. And now is angry. When he finds Alfie, sitting meditatively drinking port in the cosy warmth of the fire-corner in the bar, he looms over him, dripping wet, and cursing.

'My dear boy!' cries Alfie, 'Let me get you a whisky! And cheer up; we have our dance to look forward to, even if Ferdy has deserted us.'

'I won't be there!' William is shouting.

'Why, what are you going to do?' asks Alfie, putting the whisky in front of William.

'Secondly,' says William, downing his drink in one, and shuddering at the burning warmth down the middle of his damp and steaming self, 'I am going to take up the place on the bloody expedition to bloody St Kilda that I withdrew from because I was bloody well engaged. And firstly I'm going to get bloody pissed!'

Thomas, going through the bar in search of the reception desk, was grimly unsurprised to see Alfie. Beside him was a fellow slumped forward across the table, lost to the world, soaking wet, and giving every appearance of being blind drunk.

'Young Thomas!' said Alfie, lifting his glass by way of greeting. 'What are you doing here?'

'I'm looking for a room,' said Thomas.

'I think you'll find they have one free,' said Alfie. 'I

suppose you wouldn't consider coming to a ball with me next week? A partner having been found? Very upmarket sort of occasion?'

'No thank you,' said Thomas, 'sir. I think I would like to keep my dealings with you strictly academic. Has the great experiment gone wrong, then?'

'Well you have to remember,' said Alfie, 'that in earlier versions – you looked them all up, Thomas, didn't you? – I was a god, or at least a magician. Whereas in these latter days I can only have such power as there is in the modern world. I am only an owner. I own a house; I own a garden. I have enough money to employ people; I can pay a housekeeper to do exactly what I ask. But you rightly surmise that it isn't enough. I don't prevail.'

'And you really don't see why not?' said Thomas, looking at Alfie's insensible companion.

'No, I don't. I have never understood why the triumph of reason is so difficult,' said Alfie.

'You wouldn't know a sincere feeling if it hit you in the face!' said Thomas, warming up.

'Sincere feeling? Like yours, do you mean? My dear young man, that's not a sincere feeling, it's an act. Love takes you out of yourself, wouldn't you say? There's a cosmic script for what you're up to; with ludicrous effect it's the same script for every coupling since the dawn of time. You don't need a turban and waving mustachios to disguise you – when lovers are stark naked they are disguised from top to toe, wearing the garments of the divine, but neither loving nor loved as themselves.'

'You poor old sod,' said Thomas, 'you are not wise, only jealous!'

'No need to get abusive, dear boy,' said Alfie. 'Run along, and *act well*!'

*　　*　　*

'You wouldn't normally be lucky, sir,' says the girl at the reception desk. 'We've only got two double rooms. But tonight we have a late cancellation.' Thomas writes his name in the register, and Anna's beside his. Then he walks out again, going towards the car. As he approaches the bridge a figure emerges from the bosky woods on the bank upstream, and begins to climb the parapet, as though to jump over. Thomas runs. The figure stands upright, long dress flowing in the night breeze, arms spread, swaying. Thomas gets there, and pulls her down. He lifts her from behind, and puts her down on firm ground beside him, and holds her tight. She is wearing only an evening dress and a flower, and is freezing cold. He slips one arm out of his mac, and pulls it round her shoulders. He doesn't let go of her for a second.

'That's silly,' he says. 'Don't do that, or you won't live to regret it.'

She is sobbing convulsively, but now silently, in his grip. 'You can't know how awful it is,' she says.

'Well, you might be surprised at how good a guess I could make,' he says. 'Do you want me to go and knock someone's teeth down his throat for him?'

She suddenly seems calmer, considering it. 'Which one?' she says. 'Which one will you fight for me? Because it ought to be both or neither.'

'Ah,' says Thomas. 'Two at once might be tricky. Whose fault is it most?'

'Everyone's blaming someone else,' she says. 'But what's so awful is they won't take responsibility for what they did, what they said. I don't care who told them to do what . . . no, I don't want you to fight for me. I want to be dead.'

'Tell me what's the worst thing about it,' says Thomas, floundering. He can't leave her while she still might chuck herself in the river. He is striking out blindly; he has no idea how to talk someone out of suicide.

'It's terrifying,' she says, leaning against him, talking into his shirt. 'I'm petrified at not knowing what I feel. And not knowing what someone else feels.'

'Thinking they may be lying?' he asks. He is about to tell her that not everyone is a liar.

'No, worse. They are not lying. They really are changing between one word and the next . . . nobody means anything. Me too; my feelings too, everything dissolving and sweeping away . . . how can we live?'

And to his surprise, he understands that. 'Ah, mutability,' he says. 'Well, just don't forget that it has its up side. If nothing lasts very long, neither does misery. You'll feel better tomorrow. See if you don't. Now, do you want to go and find him, whoever it is?'

She shook her head.

'Then I'm going to get a taxi to get you home. Come on, you can't stand out here, you'll perish. Let's go in.'

The taxi has to come from Witney. Trying to keep out of sight of Alfie and his luckless drunken friend, Thomas sits the girl by the fire in the lobby, in front of the reception desk. He can see the desk clerk looking puzzled; she knows he has a room. When he brings a second girl in his reputation will be in shreds. It seems an endless age before the taxi comes, and he is worried about Anna, getting cold in the car.

At last, at last, the taxi is at the door. He hands his bedraggled, red-eyed companion into it. 'If nothing lasts for long, your luck will change!' he tells her. 'Cheer up!'

He slams the taxi door, and positively runs for the bridge.

Left alone in the car, looking out on the magical night, the river, the window light, the moonlight, Anna reaches into her bag and produces her Walkman, still containing the first tape of *Cosi*. She plays it to herself while she waits.

And listening to this music, Anna feels, is like being a desert receiving rain. There has been grander music, but never music more full of grace. No-one, she thinks, could be an audience for these ravishing arias, for they do not only portray with exquisite understanding the feelings of the characters, they vividly evoke those same feelings, making of anyone who listens each participant in turn. Washing away all resistance by its force of beauty the music makes her Fiordiligi, makes her Dorabella, makes her Guglielmo, and Ferrando, makes her Despina, and even Alfonso. While she listens she wears each mask in turn, and, it seems to her, each mask in turn does not disguise, but liberates and reveals her.

Now the lovely recorded voices are wishing sweet winds and safety to their departing lovers; now an impassioned girl is declaring herself as immovable as rock; and Anna does not believe, cannot accept, that this is the sound of false emotion. Da Ponte, no doubt, wrote an acid, clever, amusing and rationalist text, which invites her to think that what by and by proves false was false all along, in which romantic ardour of feeling is evidence of falsity. Did Mozart think that? Was Mozart writing parody, mocking the strength of first love? No, she is sure not. He is entering, accepting, blessing it with perfect expression. Perhaps the love in *Cosi* was of brief duration, but the music tells us clearly that while it lasted it was truly felt. And even the betrayals in the music do not taste bitter. One could say 'all women do it!' with contempt, with hatred of half the human race, but, as Anna thinks about Mozart, she sees there would be another way of meaning it, another tone of voice, much more probably his. Wasn't he simply trying to forgive Constanze? Wasn't he telling himself that if she flirted around in Baden, well she was no worse, after all, than anyone else. She treated him no worse than any other woman would have done, and he loved her, – *ah purtroppo!* – whatever she did.

Anna smiles to herself. This, surely, is why Mozart is called divine. If there is any divinity at work in the world, we long to think it is as tolerant, as accepting, as tenderly amused at our spectrum of feeling as he was. Anna is listening now to Fiordiligi imploring her lover to forgive her for a failing she will never – God no! – tell him about. With what depths of emotion Mozart always writes about forgiveness! '*Qui tollis peccata mundi*,' was his favourite religious text. Everyone likes *Figaro*, Anna thinks, comes out of a performance of it glowing with satisfaction, because we have been invited to forgive, and it is fun to forgive. It makes us feel superior. To forgive others you must first judge them to be in need of forgiveness. But *Cosi* leaves people feeling uncomfortable, troubled, angry even, because it invites us to take the simplest and least often attempted path, to judge not that we be not judged. But while most of us cling to judgement like a child to a dangerous toy, Mozart laughed, and blessed with irresistible beauty every successive state of our guilty, volatile and unstable hearts.

Her tape has come to an end. Her thoughts drifting, the music lingering in her mind like the fading fragrance in the rose garden, she contemplates the irreversible thrust of the river, always here, always moving. Naturally we long to be faithful. And yet 'I will love you for ever' contains a preposterous impossibility. We will not do anything for ever, or even for very long, bind ourselves how we will. But fidelity is like immortality, which all desire, whether they believe in it or not.

How well, it strikes her, that strange pair, Mozart on his way to ruin and death, Da Ponte on his way to respectability, had understood! Had seen that it is not gold, it is not rubies, it is simply love itself that is the temptation to love.

So that when Thomas returns to her, radiant with impatience, and leans down to help her out of the freezing car, swooning in his mind with thoughts of ways to warm her, she has accepted her own mutability, she has consented to everything she will ever feel for him, she is ready for ever and ever to have loved him tonight.

Acknowledgements

My grateful thanks are due to the following: Sheila Hodges, for permission to make extensive and detailed use of her *Lorenzo Da Ponte, The Life and Times of Mozart's Librettist* (Granada 1985); David Cairns, for permission to quote from *The Enigma of Cosi Fan Tutte*, The Glyndebourne Festival Programme Book (1978); J.M. Dent & Sons Ltd. for permission to quote from *Letters of Wolfgang Amadeus Mozart*, edited by Hans Mersmann, translated by M.M. Bozman (1928).

Rose names and histories are from the catalogue of Roses du Temps Passé, Woodlands House, Stretton, Nr. Stafford. I would also like to thank Ute Hitchin, who read *Da Ponte's Cosi Fan Tutte*, Kurt Kramer, Gottingen (1973) for me, and all those faithful friends who read the typescript and discussed the book with me.

J.P.W.

Knowledge Of Angels
Jill Paton Walsh

SHORTLISTED FOR THE BOOKER PRIZE 1994

'AN IRRESISTIBLE BLEND OF INTELLECT AND
PASSION . . . NOVELS OF IDEAS COME NO BETTER
THAN THIS SENSUAL EXAMPLE'
Mail on Sunday

It is, perhaps, the fifteenth century and the ordered
tranquillity of a Mediterranean island is about to be
shattered by the appearance of two outsiders: one, a
castaway, plucked from the sea by fishermen, whose
beliefs represent a challenge to the established order; the
other, a child abandoned by her mother and suckled by
wolves, who knows nothing of the precarious relationship
between church and state but whose innocence will
become the subject of a dangerous experiment.

But the arrival of the Inquisition on the island creates a
darker, more threatening force which will transform what
has been a philosophical game of chess into a matter of life
and death . . .

'A COMPELLING MEDIAEVAL FABLE, WRITTEN FROM
THE HEART AND MELDED TO A DRIVING NARRATIVE
WHICH NEVER ONCE LOSES ITS TREMENDOUS PACE'
Guardian

'THIS REMARKABLE NOVEL RESEMBLES AN
ILLUMINATED MANUSCRIPT MAPPED WITH ANGELS
AND MOUNTAINS AND SIGNPOSTS, AN ALLEGORY
FOR TODAY AND YESTERDAY TOO. A BEAUTIFUL,
UNSETTLING MORAL FICTION ABOUT VIRTUE AND
INTOLERANCE'
Observer

'REMARKABLE . . . UTTERLY ABSORBING . . . A
RICHLY DETAILED AND FINELY IMAGINED
FICTIONAL NARRATIVE'
Sunday Telegraph

0 552 99636 X

BLACK SWAN

Lapsing
Jill Paton Walsh

'A BEAUTIFULLY WRITTEN BOOK. HISTORICALLY
ACCURATE BUT NEVER SENTIMENTAL, SOLEMN BUT
NEVER STIFF, IT BUILDS QUIETLY TO UNEXPECTED
HEIGHTS'
Observer

Set in Oxford in the 1950s, *Lapsing* traces the emotional
and intellectual education of Tessa, a young woman
whose profound belief in the tenets of the church is
challenged by her love for a sensitive, tormented priest,
Theodore, troubled by physical illness and by the
demands of his calling.

Drawn to his curious blend of wisdom and innocence,
Tessa soon finds herself in a strange *ménage à trois* with a
husband she admires and the man she loves. And the
conflict which it produces forces her to confront the
foundations on which she has built her life.

'AN EXTRAORDINARY NOVEL: DELICATE, CLEVER,
SERIOUS AND FUNNY . . . RADIANT WITH
SERIOUSNESS AND PERCEPTION AND VERY CRAFTY
WRITING . . . IT HAS A WONDERFULLY INNOCENT-
SEEMING NATURALISTIC STRUCTURE WHICH
ALLOWS DEPTH AND COMPLEXITY TO SHINE
THROUGH IT'
New Statesman

'A MOST UNUSUAL LOVE STORY . . . A NOSTALGIC
AND SYMPATHETIC ACCOUNT OF LIFE IN THE PRE-
PERMISSIVE SOCIETY'
Evening Standard

'A RARE COMBINATION OF COMEDY AND
COMPASSION, PATON WALSH HAS CAPTURED
BRILLIANTLY THE EARNESTNESS AND NAIVETY OF
UNDERGRADUATE LIFE. HER LAST PARAGRAPH IS
OF SUCH BRAVE BEAUTY THAT IT MADE ME WANT
TO READ THE BOOK ALL OVER AGAIN'
Daily Telegraph

0 552 99647 5

BLACK SWAN

Dina's Book
Herbjørg Wassmo

'THE GREATNESS OF THIS BOOK IS ITS GUT-
WRENCHING PORTRAIT OF A WOMAN FOREVER IN
THE GRIP OF HER PAST'
Los Angeles Times

Set in Norway in the mid-nineteenth century – a land of
short, blazing, idyllic summers and dark, frost-rimmed
winters, of mountains, bear-hunts, and hazardous sea
voyages – *Dina's Book* centres around a beautiful,
eccentric and unpredictable woman who bewitches
everyone she meets.

At the age of five Dina unwittingly causes her mother's
death. Blamed by her father and banished to a farm, she
grows up untamed and untaught. Her guilt becomes her
obsession: her unforgiving mother haunts her every day.

When she finally returns home she is like a wolf cub,
tamed only by her tutor, Lorch, who is able to reach her
through music. Married off at sixteen to a wealthy fifty-
year-old landowner, Jacob, she becomes sexually
obsessive and wild. Jacob dies under odd circumstances
and Dina becomes mute. When finally she emerges from
her trauma, she runs his estate with an iron hand. But still
Dina wrestles with her two unappeased ghosts: Jacob and
her mother. Until one day a mysterious stranger, the
Russian wanderer, Leo, enters her life and changes it
forever . . .

'A MASTERPIECE THAT LIGHTS UP THE SKY LIKE A
MEGASTAR'
Verdens Gang, Norway

'AN EXPLOSION OF A BOOK – A UNIQUE TALENT
AND A WONDERFUL EVOCATIVE POWER'
Politken, Denmark

'A NOVEL THAT WILL STAY WITH YOU FOREVER'
Kristianstads-bladet, Sweden

0 552 99673 4

BLACK SWAN

Behind The Scenes At The Museum

Kate Atkinson

'WITHOUT DOUBT ONE OF THE FINEST NOVELS I
HAVE READ FOR YEARS'
Mary Loudon, *The Times*

Ruby Lennox was conceived grudgingly by Bunty and
born while her father, George, was in the Dog and Hare in
Doncaster telling a woman in an emerald dress and a D-
cup that he wasn't married. Bunty had never wanted to
marry George, but he was all that was left. She really
wanted to be Vivien Leigh or Celia Johnson, swept off to
America by a romantic hero. But here she was, stuck in a
flat above the pet shop in an ancient street beneath York
Minster, with sensible and sardonic Patricia aged five,
greedy cross-patch Gillian who refused to be ignored, and
Ruby . . .

Ruby tells the story of The Family, from the day at the end
of the nineteenth century when a travelling French
photographer catches frail beautiful Alice and her
children, like flowers in amber, to the startling, witty, and
memorable events of Ruby's own life.

'WRITTEN WITH AN EXTRAORDINARY PASSION . . .
PACKED WITH IMAGES OF BEWITCHING POTENCY,
THIS IS AN ASTOUNDING BOOK'
The Times

'WITTY AND ORIGINAL . . . . A REMARKABLE DEBUT
NOVEL'
Daily Mirror

'ENCHANTING. IT HOPS WITH SPRIGHTLY
OMNISCIENCE FROM PAST TO FUTURE AND BACK
AGAIN'
Sunday Times

'A FIRST NOVEL WRITTEN SO FLUENTLY AND
WITTILY THAT I SAILED THROUGH IT AS THOUGH
BLOWN BY AN EXHILARATING WIND. I LOVED IT'
Margaret Forster

0 552 99618 1

BLACK SWAN

A SELECTED LIST OF FINE WRITING AVAILABLE FROM BLACK SWAN

THE PRICES SHOWN BELOW WERE CORRECT AT THE TIME OF GOING TO PRESS. HOWEVER TRANSWORLD PUBLISHERS RESERVE THE RIGHT TO SHOW NEW RETAIL PRICES ON COVERS WHICH MAY DIFFER FROM THOSE PREVIOUSLY ADVERTISED IN THE TEXT OR ELSEWHERE.

99618 1	BEHIND THE SCENES AT THE MUSEUM	Kate Atkinson	£6.99
99588 6	THE HOUSE OF THE SPIRITS	Isabel Allende	£6.99
99648 3	TOUCH AND GO	Elizabeth Berridge	£5.99
99531 2	AFTER THE HOLE	Guy Burt	£5.99
99537 1	GUPPIES FOR TEA	Marika Cobbold	£5.99
99587 8	LIKE WATER FOR CHOCOLATE	Laura Esquivel	£5.99
99602 5	THE LAST GIRL	Penelope Evans	£5.99
99622 X	THE GOLDEN YEAR	Elizabeth Falconer	£5.99
99488 X	SUGAR CAGE	Connie May Fowler	£5.99
99599 1	SEPARATION	Dan Franck	£5.99
99616 5	SIMPLE PRAYERS	Michael Golding	£5.99
99610 6	THE SINGING HOUSE	Janette Griffiths	£5.99
99609 2	FORREST GUMP	Winston Groom	£5.99
99590 8	OLD NIGHT	Clare Harkness	£5.99
99538 X	GOOD AS GOLD	Joseph Heller	£6.99
99605 X	A SON OF THE CIRCUS	John Irving	£7.99
99567 3	SAILOR SONG	Ken Kesey	£6.99
99542 8	SWEET THAMES	Matthew Kneale	£6.99
99130 9	NOAH'S ARK	Barbara Trapido	£6.99
99549 5	A SPANISH LOVER	Joanna Trollope	£6.99
99636 X	KNOWLEDGE OF ANGELS	Jill Paton Walsh	£5.99
99647 5	LAPSING	Jill Paton Walsh	£5.99
99673 4	DINA'S BOOK	Herbjørg Wassmo	£6.99
99592 4	AN IMAGINATIVE EXPERIENCE	Mary Wesley	£5.99
99639 4	THE TENNIS PARTY	Madeleine Wickham	£5.99
99591 6	A MISLAID MAGIC	Joyce Windsor	£4.99